"I DON'T HAPPEN T... BEING YOUR DAUGHTER TODAY!"

"That's pretty difficult, you know, Tessa," her father said. "Turning on and off like that. Don't I even get any warning?"

"Why should you? We never get any. Mother gets up and announces that today she's got plans and we're on our own. Which we're not. Today, one day a week, we're supposed to be your children. Terrific!"

"I understand how you feel, Tessa, but maybe you don't realize that it's upsetting and painful for me too."

"Then how could you do this, all this talk about remarriage, without even thinking once about us, about Allie and me? Instead you just hand it to me! Don't you ever stop to think about anybody but yourself?"

"Tessa," her father warned, "I'm perfectly happy to discuss all this with you, as long as you remember who you are and who I am."

"Oh, that's terrific coming from you! You only remember once a week yourself . . . !"

Sunday Father

SIGNET Books You'll Enjoy Reading

SUNDAY FATHER

by John Neufeld

A SIGNET BOOK from

NEW AMERICAN LIBRARY

TIMES MIRROR

Published by
THE NEW AMERICAN LIBRARY
OF CANADA LIMITED

NAL Books are also available at discounts in bulk quantity for industrial or sales-promotional use. For details, write to Premium Marketing Division, New American Library, Inc., 1301 Avenue of the Americas, New York, New York 10019.

First Signet Printing, January, 1977

1 2 3 4 5 6 7 8 9

 SIGNET TRADEMARK REG. U.S. PAT. OFF. AND FOREIGN COUNTRIES
REGISTERED TRADEMARK — MARCA REGISTRADA
HECHO EN WINNIPEG, CANADA

SIGNET, SIGNET CLASSICS, MENTOR, PLUME AND MERIDIAN BOOKS are published in Canada by The New American Library of Canada Limited, Scarborough, Ontario

PRINTED IN CANADA
COVER PRINTED IN U.S.A.

Sunday Father

1.

Now it hits me! If I'd looked at my brother's face, especially at his eyes, I would have known. I'd have guessed Allie'd discovered a way of taking someone in, a way of getting something for nothing.

Still, it isn't my fault, not really. I wasn't thinking about Dad just then. Or about what's been happening to our lives this past year.

But Allie's like that, taking you by surprise. He looks angelic—all freckled and sandy-haired with hardly any nose at all, and big innocent blue-green eyes that he uses as though they were the most precious promise or gift he could ever offer. He does that only because my dad once told him that when he meets someone for the first time, he's supposed to shake hands firmly and look the other person straight in the eye, without blinking, to show honesty and good will. By now Allie's got this down to a science.

If you know Allie at all, you can see when he means something and when he doesn't. When he's up to some weird or slippery surprise, when he has some truly bizarre plan of action in mind, all you have to do is put him under the brightest light you can find and look at his eyes. If they're more green than blue, then it's time to worry!

Which I should have noticed, just now. And didn't.

And I wasn't daydreaming, either, or gazing out the windows. Our view where we live now isn't that great anyway. We can't see, as you can from Daddy's apartment, the mountains, just now in November snow-capped

7

and seeming even bigger than before, as though they were daring a wagon train all over again to cross them. You can also see, from Daddy's place, all of downtown Denver, which isn't as thrilling as New York, maybe, or even Chicago, but at night, when you can't quite figure out whether Denver's a huge city or a small town with a few tall buildings, it's still pretty impressive.

The reason I didn't happen to catch on to Allie's act right away was that I was racing through my homework so that by the time my friend Charlotte arrived it would be finished. You wouldn't believe it, but before I can do anything around here I have to prove, just as if I were in court, that everything I'm supposed to do, I've done. My mother's excuse for this incredible behavior is that now, since she's alone, she has to be both mother and father to us, and that this may sometimes mean a little more discipline. *Sometimes!*

Anyway, I was in a panic. Charlotte's due any minute *with* her sleeping bag, and the late show is absolutely to die over (so *she* says) and we won't want to miss a minute of it. Don't ask why the sleeping bag. Charlotte thinks if she's outdoorsy and woodsy and "game," boys will like her more. In fact, boys don't like her at all. She doesn't know when to shut up, or when to give in, or when even to behave like a girl. Backpacking and hiking and rock-climbing and skiing and all that make her seem to be challenging everyone. And she is.

Actually, to be truthful, there's another reason for the sleeping bag. In our new "house," there isn't any room for extra people to stay overnight. My mother and I share a room, and Allie gets his own little hide-out. One bathroom, a small kitchen, and a living room is all that's left. So if I ask someone over, they either have to bring a sleeping bag or sleep on chair cushions on the floor. The convertible couch Mother's ordered hasn't arrived yet.

Enough. What matters is trying to outguess Allie before it's too late. Before Dad comes to pick us up tomorrow, which is Sunday and his "specified" day to be with us now, and finds he's being worked over, or on.

The alarm I *didn't* hear was very clear in the evening air. Allie bounces into my room without knocking (why should he change now?), throws himself on the rug, and proceeds to be very nonchalant and palsy. I sensed all this rather than saw. Sometimes, if you take no notice of someone, he disappears. He sprawls silent a moment, building suspense probably. Then he asks it outright. "Do you ever feel guilty, Tessa?"

I didn't bother to answer. Sooner or later everyone feels guilty about something.

"What I mean is," he explained rather superciliously (my favorite new word), "do you ever feel guilty about what happened between Mom and Dad?"

I was tempted to turn and say, "Oh, for God's sakes, Allie!" which I'm crazy about doing when Mother isn't around. I decided instead to enter the Supercilious Sweepstakes. "Ohhh," I said, stretching out the word without looking down at him (my mistake!), "that's just infantile!"

"Mom and Dad don't think so," he said.

"Ummm," was all I offered, being just then within four pages of finishing an assigned book.

"They're worried that we might be feeling guilty. *Responsible*," he tacked on, accenting the word as though it opened locked doors or brought genies out of lamps.

"Allie, if you don't mind," I said, still not turning in my chair, "I'd be thrilled to talk Freud with you. Some other time."

"What's Freud?"

I made a truly disgusting sound and waved at him to get out of my inner sanctum. Which he did. Which was another mistake.

Because, now that I think of it, I don't know whether or not I feel guilty over the divorce, *or* responsible. I was sad, of course. And I felt bad for both Mom and Dad. But I figured I was old enough to handle it. I mean, I already knew kids whose parents had split, so it wasn't such a big thing. Two people don't get along anymore and they separate. It makes perfect sense, really. I *was* surprised. I have to admit that. But guilty? It never really occurred to me.

It does now. Mostly because it must have occurred to Allie. And *that* could be dangerous.

You see, I don't think there's an honest bone in Allie's body. He's very cool, I mean *very* cool for an eleven-year-old. For example, in all that stuff about Watergate you kept running into all those terrifically cool guys who had no emotions, no sense of right or wrong. Allie's like that. It's not just that he's my brother, or that sometimes we don't get on so sensationally. He's a planner, an organizer, a manipulator (which is another of my favorite words, although mostly I use it to describe other girls in my class).

Not that he's precriminal or anything. What I'm trying to say is that Allie's very, very cautious. You can see him thinking, weighing things in his mind: if I do that, what will happen? Maybe I should do the other. Maybe that would get me more. Further. Faster.

I'm sure he was an adorable baby.

Which leads me back to what sort of deal he's cooking up now. It has to do with being guilty. Or pretending, at least, to feel guilty. But so what? I don't know that anyone ever got ahead by *pretending* to be sorry for something.

But there isn't time now to think it all through. Charlotte will be here in a second and the movie starts almost instantly. I know I'll never be able to concentrate on whatever the trap is Allie's laying in time for Daddy's visit.

So I'll just have to keep watch on old Green Eyes. The minute I can see what he's up to, I'll tip off Daddy. It isn't fair being embarrassed by your own son. Or being taken for a ride.

You know what I hate? I hate it when someone puts an idea into your mind that you hadn't planned to think about, and then you can't stop.

Apart from the fact that the movie Charlotte's hypnotized by is a bomb, and boring and dumb, right now I can't think of anything else but the divorce. And guilt.

I'll tell you something, though. Or half of something. I'm not *going* to think about the divorce. And to keep my mind off that particular fable (as well as to get away from *The Legend of Lylah Clare,* which has a lot of people in it you hardly ever hear about anymore, like Kim Novak), here I stand in our dumpy kitchen stirring hot chocolate.

"Dumpy" is a pretty accurate word. Our new home, such as it is, would be perfect for newlyweds just starting out who don't really care where they live as long as it's together. But for three people, one of them Allie, it's impossible.

The real problem, the thing that gets to me the most, is that this really isn't ours at all. What we *had* was ours.

We used to live over on the 6th Avenue Parkway, just east of Colorado. Which, if you know Denver at all, is sort of grand. Actually, it's an odd street. All along the Parkway are these terrifically beautiful houses, some of them a lot more like manor houses or chateaux than just houses for ordinary American people. And then, just off, on the cross streets, the houses get very small. Neat, but more like the cottages of medieval serfs. Now that I've said that, I know it really isn't fair. I mean, some of the smaller places *are* cute.

Anyway, our house was at the corner of the Parkway and Forest Street, a sort of mix between Norman castle and fake Tudor, with a lot of brickwork and some beautiful, huge evergreens. The only dismal thing about it was that right in front of the house was a bus stop. I mean, that was great for me, since you have to be six-teen to drive in Colorado, but it was also great for people's maids.

So there you are, walking home with someone you might even be interested in (moderately), catching your first sight of The Residence, and there stand three or four domestics in ratty cloth coats at the curbside looking eastward for a big, noisy, dirty bus to come along. It didn't do a lot for property value. (The lady from Billings and Co., the real-estate people Daddy got hold of to sell the house, thought, on the other hand, that the bus stop was a "positive feature of the layout." Especially with the gas shortage and all.)

Now, I don't want to give the impression that what we had was (in real-estate argot) a "showplace." It *looked* bigger than it actually was. It may even have been more than we should have had. Because, accord-ing to my father, he was "killing" himself to keep it. (At fourteen you *do* get wind of things like that.) Which of course made him sometimes short and angry. Which of course made Mother defensive and quick. Which naturally made Daddy impatient and loud. Which might have made Mother conciliatory. But didn't.

(One of my favorite words is "escalation.")

But what mattered most then, and matters now looking back, is that whatever was happening there was happening in our house. It was *ours*. Period.

Right now, standing on brownish scarred tile before an old gas range (gas!) and stirring Nestle's, right now we're living in someone else's house. No matter how good a face my mother puts on it, the fact is basic. We live in a two-family house!

I don't mean to sound snobbish and snotty. But how can one exist surrounded by people who, no matter how hard they try not to, still can't help overhearing what you say, or smelling what you're having for dinner, or tracking your progress around the house by listening to your footsteps above?

From the outside 2341 Ash Street doesn't look half-bad. You can hardly tell it's a duplex. It's all painted white brick, and it has neat black shutters at its windows. It has a New Englandish kind of shape and a black wrought-iron lamp fixture above the front door. (*Our* entrance is off the driveway, at the back of the house.)

According to my mother on her hyperenthusiastic days, there are a million reasons why it's just perfect for us all.

(1) I don't have to change schools. Which doesn't make sense at all, because, though I still spend most of my time at East High, bussing is a feature of living in Denver and you never know when you're going to be carted away, or where you're going to end up.

(2) I can keep all my old friends, plus make new ones in a new neighborhood. Which is to say, according to my mother, my "horizons" are too limited and shouldn't be. Where we live now is Park Hill, which is all integrated and mixed up and very proud of itself for being that way.

(3) Allie will have a chance, next year, to go to a new junior high school. Terrific. Where we were he would have had the same chance. That is, if they ever finish building the school at all.

(4) There's a Colonel Sanders not more than five minutes away, which is fine if you like chicken (Allie does).

(5) Now that we're "alone," having very close

neighbors (close!) makes my mother feel more secure.

(6) The move was "sensible." Which means, I guess, that Mother feels she got about as much as she could expect from Daddy and that she's determined to make it all stretch as far as possible.

If you stop to think about all this for a minute, you can hear the reasons beneath the reasons. A move like this is less disruptive for the children; it makes sense financially; and, most important, it means Mother doesn't have to stay in our old neighborhood and be pitied by all her lady friends or, worse, move into a development (like Crestmoor Park) and feel deprived and lonely or, worst of all, move to the "suburbs" in the southeast and get a lot of flack under the guise of interest and sympathy from all the ladies still (they think) happily married and sealed like cement into their husbands' lives.

One more reason. Moving into Park Hill, which is "committed," means that Mother can start a life over again, getting involved in all kinds of new things in order to meet new people and make new friends. For example, this very night while Charlotte and I are supposed to be sitting with Allie, she's off at a meeting of the Greater Park Hill Committee, in theory doing "good works."

Actually, what's going on over there is a wine-tasting party, which certainly sounds better and more fun than sitting in a smoky room all night long worrying about property values and taxes and street maintenance.

Anyway, while we three put smiles on our faces every morning and pretend to whistle, naturally my father lucks out. He's a counsel for Martin-Marietta, which is this huge company that makes all sorts of things for space projects and airplanes and so on, and which also, happily for Daddy, just happens to keep a splendiferous apartment at No. 2 Cheesman Place.

The idea is that Martin-Marietta can entertain there,

or put up visiting dignitaries, or important executives who travel with their wives. The thing is, though, that with the economy and all, the place is hardly used because no one wants to spend the money to fly around for meetings when the telephone is cheaper and makes more sense. So, Daddy was allowed to move into this enormous glass-and-marble place with a view of all downtown and beyond, into the mountains, overlooking the park. It's very grand, and about the best thing that happens now to Allie and me is that on Sundays sometimes we end up our visits there and have dinner sent in and watch television until it's time to be "returned."

One amazing thing: it took so very little time for all our lives to be changed so much.

It was only eight months ago that my parents decided to separate. But I guess that must have been their roughest decision because, once that was done, everything else moved like sixty. One day my mother announced that she was off to the Dominican Republic. It was very mysterious and very jet-setty, which of course is all wrong for her to begin with. She didn't tell us then what the real reason for the trip was, but gave us a lot of what seemed mystifying talk about how a change of scene would brighten her spirits and stuff like that.

When she returned, it was all over. There's a divorce mill down there on the island, and I guess you arrive, spend one night, show up in court the next morning and nod a lot (unless you know the language), and then the judge says O.K., it's all over, you're free, you can go home now. (In a lot of old movies they show on television, people are always going to Reno. But I investigated that; you have to stay around there six weeks before you can get your divorce. After almost sixteen years, I guess six weeks more was just too much for Mother.)

So, she comes back home; the house has a "For Sale, Exclusive" sign planted on its front lawn; three more weeks and it's done—we're in Park Hill, Allie's developing new schemes for God knows what, and I suddenly have become a little more interesting in school.

Now, I'm not all that crazy about Women's Lib, but I have to say I think Mother got the worst of the deal. I mean, she and Daddy were married in their senior years at Boulder. In those days, it was the thing to do. When my father decided to go on to law school, it was Mother who worked to keep him there, financially. Even when Allie and I came along, we had nurses so that my mother could keep working. (What happened was that Mother worked for a bank and what we had really weren't nurses and nannies but a succession of girls from the University who needed a place to stay free and who didn't mind baby-sitting and fixing bottles and changing diapers.)

Later, when we moved into Denver, my mother stopped working because Dad figured that *his* wife shouldn't be seen in any kind of socially compromising position. The thought occurs to me now: if he felt that way, why did she work even after he had his first job with a law firm in Boulder? Anyway, Mother was glad to stop, because by then she had to get us into and through school, and you *know* what that means. Car pools and den-mothering and homeroom-mothering and P.T.A. meetings and country clubs (though this, too, was frequently accused of "killing" Daddy) and hobby shops and Red Cross and the United Fund and who knows what all. Which is to say that while my mother was freed, in a way, she was instantly chained to all kinds of new ideas and projects for our sakes or for the sake of my father's job.

The point of all this is just to show that while Mother learned how to be a Class A Helpmate in nothing flat, she never had time to do anything *she* might actually like doing.

She still doesn't. I think she *thinks* she does. "Just think, Tessa," came at me twelve times a day for a while, "when so many important things can be done in this world, what a wonderful opportunity we all have now to be *involved*." I mean, this sounds suspiciously like convincing *yourself,* if you know what I mean.

You see, I'm not totally certain what's expected of Allie and me. We *are* involved. He's got all his swindles and subterfuges, and I've got all the problems of being fourteen, which is no slim agenda.

There's ecology, I suppose, and politics if you're blind, deaf, and dumb. Art, which does interest me in a secret sort of way; civic pride (which would mean more if we'd ever been anywhere but Kansas City, where our grandparents live—it would help to be able to compare Denver with more other cities). Still, even before we'd moved, these "opportunities" were on my mother's lips from the time she woke till the time she went to bed. Actually, I felt a little sorry for her even then because Allie and I just can't be reasonably expected to share all her hot new ideas and plans. I mean, no matter where we live or what we do, we still have to go to school and pass everything and somehow manage to be a credit to our family. This doesn't leave a lot of time for trying to accomplish important things in the world.

There is one thing in all this, though, that does make me angry. Neither Allie nor I was ever shown our "new house" until the day we moved in. My mother knew what she wanted and how much and where and then did it, period. If my father was never aware of his selfishness with Mother, she's not keenly aware of her own, now, with us, either.

Charlotte has just announced that "the good part"

is coming. What that means, I gather, is a gory part where Lylah kills a rapist, or maybe it's later, when she falls from a trapeze (Charlotte is constitutionally unable not to tell you in advance what to watch for). It doesn't make any difference to me, but for Charlotte's sake I'll go in and make the appropriate excited-sounding noises and comments. With the hot chocolate.

And then, finally, when all is quiet and serene and dark, I won't be able to sleep at all, worrying about what Allie has planned for tomorrow.

One of the things I'd like to change about my life, if you want to know, is my dad. He visits us every Sunday and takes us places. I'm convinced he feels he has to make every Sunday some sort of special holiday or outing for us. Well, this child would really rather just have lunch somewhere and bum around, maybe dropping in at the Celebrity Sports Center (even though mostly what you get there are retarded teeny-boppers) or at Baskin-Robbins or maybe going to a movie and wolfing down buttered popcorn by the quart ("double-butter, please"). But always, every Sunday morning, Daddy calls and builds his act up, tells us what to wear, how to prepare, what to expect. The act is divided into three kinds of "treats": Something Educational, like going to the Natural History Museum (which we do with our classes, for God's sake!); Something Athletic (skiing, if you can believe it!); Something Cultural, like seeing a play at the Auditorium Theater because, according to *both* my parents, we should at least be aware of the "magic of live theater."

We always eat well on Sundays, of course, but what a strain to keep conversation going brightly. What a relief it would be to wear jeans and sneakers and spend a whole afternoon just rummaging around Buckingham Square and eating awful food and laughing and window-shopping and then, maybe, to come back to Daddy's place at No. 2, kick off our shoes and eat

Chinese food in front of the 25-inch set there and go into a trance of well-being without thinking.

I'm not at all sure people understand how difficult it is, how much of a performer a kid has to be to survive.

2.

Tessa O'Connell slid to a stop, dodging other skiers who, ahead of her, had gotten off the lift. Her father skied down a few yards to his left, turned, and looked up at Tessa, waiting for her.

But Tessa didn't move. She had realized with a sudden chill that Allie wasn't behind them.

The idea of his being lost, itself, didn't come to her as quickly as the idea that Allie must have taken off somewhere on his own, and that it was nearly three-thirty, time for a last run, with shadows swiftly lowering on the hills and the light going fast.

It was a dangerous time to ski at best, and at worst stupid: your legs were about to give out any moment, you were sweating and probably an inch away from pneumonia, and you took extra chances all for the sake of one last headlong dive down a mountainside, trying for a run that afterward you could boast of and remember as more dangerous and hair-raising than it really was.

Her father began inching his way back up the slope toward where Tessa stood craning to see if Allie were on his way up. Out of the corner of her eye, Tessa saw her father stepping choppily, avoiding the heedless shouting dashes of last-minute hot-doggers. It was easy to

spot Mr. O'Connell: he was more than six feet tall and
he wore a green felt Tyrolean hat with one single long
pheasant feather in its band.

Allie was more difficult to find, being short and
rolled into a dark green parka, blue jeans, and a pair
of goggles. There were, Tessa estimated, only five hundred other kids at Winter Park that day who looked
exactly the same.

"Tessa?" called her father, stopping on the other side
of the lift's runout and waving at her. "Are you coming?"

Tessa nodded, half yes, half no. Then it came to her
that perhaps Allie was implementing whatever the
scheme was he had come up with the previous day. He
had said nothing more about guilt or responsibility, but
that was only typical of him: he sat on things, in his
mind, and turned them every which way before he
acted.

Nothing would be easier for him to have decided than
to escape or hide or run away here, camouflaged by
thousands of whizzing figures and shouts and lift lines
and evergreen trees that now, as she looked up the
mountain, seemed marshaled to protect the missing
boy, as though they had been planted and grown only
to be a protective screen, something behind which he
could hide as long as he wished undetected.

But why would he want to disappear this way?

"You go on, Daddy," Tessa called suddenly, miming
that her father should turn and start down the trail
behind him. "I'll meet you at the bottom!"

Without waiting for a response, Tessa started poling
and began soon to slide easily down the ice-crusted run
toward a lift that would take her up the second half
of the slope. She turned, seeing her father watching her
a second before turning and leaping off to start his run
down the hill. After all, she reasoned to herself, there's

no reason for him to worry about me. I'm a perfectly capable skier and I'm fourteen in any case, an adult.

She edged across an icy patch and continued her short run to the Apollo lift. What could be in the back of Allie's mind? Of course, there was the possibility, slight but real, that he had merely decided to ski alone, or even with someone he'd met on the mountain he knew from school.

Tessa herself, while she loved her father, frequently was conscious of missed opportunities as she went up and down the hills with her father as sole companion. After all, if she were standing alone in lift lines, there was always the chance she'd be able to ride up the mountain with some supersensational boy. (She never allowed herself to fantasize beyond this one happy, wholesome meeting. Romance in advance she had decided was no romance at all. If you imagined everything that could happen to you, there was no real reason to let it happen. You had already been through it. And besides, why be disappointed when what really happened wasn't nearly as much fun or as intriguing as what you had imagined would happen?)

Then again, if Allie had wanted to ski off with a pal, he could have told them. Couldn't he? Unless he hadn't wanted to. Hadn't wanted, at first, to be missed.

Oh! That little creep! Of course!

There were only twenty people standing in line for the lift, and before Tessa had much more time to think about where Allie might have chosen to hide out, let alone why, she was standing at the runway, her head turned to see the chair coming up quickly behind her, and then, with a sudden lurch, she was lifted into the air, her legs with boots and skis attached swinging sharply up and then back, and she was riding to the mountain's top ridge, alone.

She watched skiers on both her left and right as she traveled upward, not consciously thinking "Oh, there he is!" or "Nope, not that one." If Allie was off somewhere, snuggling into a snow den or under pines, he would have first to get to wherever it was he felt safe. If Allie were sensible, Tessa decided, he'd stay out of sight somewhere near the bottom of the hill so that, if he wasn't rescued before dark, he could at least ski down the mountain later safely. But Allie wasn't sensible.

And—oh! it made her so mad to think what he was doing! It was so mean, unmerciful; so unkind. She felt sorry for her father, left alone on the mountain, skiing down alone, expecting at the bottom to meet his kids and drive back into Denver, stopping somewhere along the way for hamburgers or fried chicken. It was so cruel of Allie to do this. And so unnecessary.

After all, if he was only pretending to be upset or angry or frustrated, if he didn't really feel guilty or responsible, couldn't he understand how much this would hurt their father? How much it would make *him* feel guilty and responsible and, at least until Allie were "found," how much a failure? Of course, Tessa understood quickly: Allie *could* understand all this. Why else would he pull this kind of stunt?

She could see the runout approaching and she leaned forward in her chair, her hands at both sides of the seat to help ease her body onto the snow, her poles held in one hand and wide of her body as she pushed herself off the chair and away and skied easily down the few feet to a level resting area. She adjusted her goggles, looking around. The few skiers behind her followed her onto the snow that now had a hard crust of ice and steered quickly around her, disappearing off onto the mountainside on one of the many trails that began at the peak.

How impossible this was, she decided. How could she begin to guess where Allie had gone? The late-afternoon light was failing, turning flat as though pushed down into the snow by the winds that whipped across the mountain's crest from the southwest. If she took the easiest way down the mountain, she'd be missing all the little cutoffs and surprise trails on which it would be so easy to hide. All the time she would be pushing and poling and sliding around moguls, Tessa felt certain Allie would be somewhere else, maybe able from where he was to look at her searching, laughing under his breath and hoping all the while she'd take a huge spill.

All right, then. She'd have to ski both the easy and the difficult trails. She could start at the top of Phipps, slide over to Dormouse, take the Vista Dome cutoff, and then edge her cautious way through the trees to Engeldive, holding her breath all the while. If she came down slowly, assuming the light held and was good enough, she would have a better chance at guessing where Allie was, at spotting his parka behind some trees or over a hill somewhere where there were no ski tracks. That would be just like him: skiing where no one else had ever gone before, regardless of the fact that he knew, that instructors had told them all, never to ski alone where no tracks could be seen. Rocks, fallen trees covered over, ravines. One could never be sure. Until, of course, one lay on one's back somewhere, a bent leg twisted unnaturally and no one within shouting distance to help.

She looked at her wristwatch. If she didn't hurry, she'd be lost in shadows and darkness herself. Besides, she was freezing.

She slid off to a confluence of trails, looking over the lips of the hills ahead of her, trying to decide again. No matter what way she chose, she would have to move slowly, stopping every few yards to look both to her right and left, scanning the trails that flanked her own, paying particular attention to any clumps of free-standing pines, to the trees that grew alongside lift lines, to any sudden curves in trails that could shield a tiny fugitive around a corner.

Well, it might be rather nice, skiing this late in the day, not having to worry about someone barreling down on top of·you, forgetting to yell "Track!" or even "Watch out!" You could take time to stop above a sea of moguls and never feel as though you were being pushed from behind to shove off into them before you were totally prepared. You wouldn't have to ski around fallen bodies, or watch out for little kids, or worry about colliding in midslope as you eased across an icy patch. You might even be able to sing a little out loud, if you wanted to, in rhythm with your own body's motion and not feel embarrassed at all.

Tessa pushed off, sliding forward, edging her skis into the mountainside in order to keep control. Her whole effort would be wasted if somewhere along the line she was suddenly out of control, skiing too fast and whizzing by trees and meeting trails and unable to stop in time to examine the terrain on all sides of her. She was smiling as she felt herself rise slightly and then dip into her first turn, an easy swing to the right, and begin a twenty-yard drop down the first stretch of slope, and as she stopped then, pulled off her goggles, and looked around.

Above her no other skier stood watching. It was an almost eerie sensation to be so alone. And rather exciting. She sidestepped a bit rightward and looked into a scrawny, windblown clump of scrub pine. She saw nothing that interested her immediately, but she stood a moment more, peering at the landscape, thinking she might catch sight of a telltale clue.

The cold and the sweeping wind were more than Allie could stand, just hanging around on the deck of the base house. He turned, hunch-shouldered, and clomped back into the emptied building, looking enviously and vainly at the cafeteria area, closed. His father had told him to stay on the deck, waiting. He had done so. But enough was enough.

What a dumb thing, anyway. Combing the mountainside for one silly girl, who probably had already hitched a ride or something back into town. Tessa was like that: impulsive. She never told you what you really needed to know, and afterward, she'd say as cooly as you please, "But even *you,* Allie, could grasp that simple idea." That is, she'd say that if what she was trying to announce made any sense. If it didn't, or if it wasn't the real reason she'd done something really gross, she'd get huffy and "sophisticated" and just wave at you as though you were the lowest, least important speck on the face of the earth.

The sound of his heavy boots on the wooden planks echoed coldly around him. Allie waved his hands and blew on them, and walked back to the windows that ran along the west edge of the building, looking out into almost pitch dark. If Tessa didn't turn up soon, maybe they'd get to stay in a motel somewhere overnight so they could start looking again at dawn. That would be pretty exciting.

He should have asked his father for some money. There were a few vending machines at the cafeteria's edge, and a hot-chocolate or even a coffee with cream and sugar would help him keep warm. But he'd forgotten. Not forgotten, really, but rather hadn't thought about it when he watched his father getting so excited and worried. He had tried to reassure his father, telling him that the last skiers weren't off the mountain yet and that Tessa would surely be coming soon. But his father had been instantly certain that this wouldn't happen. That something had happened to her, that she'd gotten lost or had taken a bad spill and couldn't get help. The mountain was nearly empty when his father had become alarmed, and truthfully, Allie admitted, if Tessa was standing around with a broken leg somewhere (he smiled: *lying* around somewhere), with the slopes empty and darkness falling it might be pretty scary.

As for himself, all he could do was wait and feel sort of silly. The last employees of the mountain were packing it in for the day, turning off lights, locking doors, bundling up, and passing him every now and then headed for their cars in the lot outside. Pretty soon he'd be all alone. Maybe someone would even tell him to leave, to wait outside.

Well, if that happened, he'd just have to hope for mercy. He could tell the truth, that his sister was lost on the hill somewhere and that the patrol and his father were out hunting for her. But he doubted that would really make someone feel bad. He might have to cry, just a little. Well, he could, if he wanted.

He clunked over the hardwood floor toward the double doors that led outward and there waited, peering through the glass. He looked up to the top of Upper Hughes, one of his favorite trails—wide and tough and embarrassing to older people when a kid like himself skied circles around them. They pretended to ignore you, of course, or sometimes shouted something angry at you, but secretly you knew they really wanted to do exactly the same things, to ski exactly as well and effortlessly and naturally as you did.

No one moved on the mountainside before him. This part of the terrain hadn't to be searched because, after all, his father had watched Tessa ski off to the Apollo lift, which was far to the north, around some trees, and besides, while she could have come down one of the expert trails to her left, she wouldn't have. Also, the ski patrol had already combed that part of the hill, as they did every afternoon. So it was decided Tessa had probably gotten off Apollo, or maybe Prospector and headed north again, coming down a baby slope like Phipps or maybe even Kendrick, which was about the longest run on the whole mountain.

The rescue operation was going on where Allie could only wait, not see, and boredom attended his vigil.

It would be interesting to hear Tessa explain this one, he thought. No doubt she would try somehow to blame the whole thing on him, Allie. That was the way she was. Whenever she didn't want to do something special, that maybe Mom or his father had asked, the reason was Allie. And whenever she had already done something that was guaranteed to send the parents up the wall, the reason for this too was Allie. He sighed. Tessa was his own personal cross.

A movement in the shadows at his right caught his eye and Allie leaned toward the window to peer out at it. His father was sliding to a sloppy stop near the ski racks. Allie pushed open a door and clambered down the steps.

"Is it all over?" he asked as he stood on the walkway just below the early-season snow.

His father shook his head, the feather in his hat bobbing like a broken reed in a wind. "There's just no sign of her, Allie," said Mr. O'Connell sadly.

"Then what are you doing here?" Allie asked. "Are you giving up?" The real idea that something *had* happened to his sister caused a confusion in Allie. Half of him said neat-o, what a story this is for the guys, and he was almost beginning to run a film in his own mind of Tessa's funeral when a cold chill of concern and worry came over him, and a sadness.

His father stepped out of his bindings and half-jumped down onto the sidewalk. "Of course we're not giving up," he said. "But the patrol thought I should get off the mountain. They had enough trouble, they said, worrying about Tessa without forever looking over their shoulders to see if *I* was O.K. Or maybe even lost, too, in the darkness."

Allie waited. "Besides," said his father, "they saw me take a pretty silly fall up on White Rabbit."

"Ohhh," said Allie, nodding, understanding the whys and wherefores of a ski patrol stakeout better than his father.

"Is there anything warm left in there?" his father asked, putting his arm over Allie's shoulder and turning him back around toward the warming house.

"There's some stuff in machines," Allie said. "If you've got any change."

They walked up the stairs and into the deserted building. Allie motioned, pointing out the concessions that could still be used, and his father bought them both hot chocolates.

They moved toward the front of the warming house, sitting on a long wooden bench that looked out now into total darkness. "I don't know why I let her go," said Allie's father, shaking his head sadly.

Allie was half-tempted to play dumb and say, "You mean Mom?", but he didn't. The furrows in his father's forehead, and the sadness in his voice, stopped him. But he wasn't certain what he *should* say. He could be hopeful, or sympathetic, or just neutral. He watched his father pull off his mittens and start to slap them into the palm of one hand. "The whole ridiculous thing is my fault," said his father.

"But why?" Allie asked. "Tessa's the one who went off and disappeared."

"But I should have stopped her," said his father. "It was late. We all know enough not to overski, or hang on to a last run for too long." He paused, looking sideways at Allie as he lifted his plastic cup of chocolate to his mouth. "That's the only reason I'm here with you, now," he said. "I'm beat, just beat. And the ski patrol could see it. That's why I fell."

"Are you gonna call Mom?" Allie asked.

His father put down his chocolate. "Not yet, Allie," he answered. "We don't want to do that yet."

"Besides, why worry her?" Allie said somberly, inwardly pleased with the sound of his own "adult" words.

His father smiled.

"You gonna punish Tessa?" Allie asked suddenly, in a second forgetting his pose in favor of a little glee-in-advance.

"The first thing is to find her," his father said. "That's all that matters now, getting her back safely and in one piece. And making sure she's all right. She must be freezing out there on that hill."

Allie was disappointed, a little, inside. He opted instead for what his parents called "common sense." "Maybe you should go get the car, then," he said. "You could warm it up, get the heat turned on and really running strong. I bet you could drive it right in here, right up to the pro shop, if you wanted."

"What I should be doing," replied his father in an anguished voice, "is hunting out there on that mountain for her. That's what I should be doing!" He stood suddenly and drained the last of the hot chocolate. "Christ in heaven, I feel so guilty, so stupid!"

"It's not your fault," Allie said, standing almost as quickly as his father. "You're not responsible for every dumb thing Tessa does."

"For this I am," his father said. "She's in my care. She's my daughter. She's my little girl!"

Mr. O'Connell pulled a mitten on as he started for the doors to the outside shadow world.

"Where are you going?" called Allie. "You can't ski *up* the hill!"

"I can be there at the bottom, though, when they come down. When Tessa comes down," said his father, taking a step toward the door and reaching out for a handle.

"What about me?" Allie wanted to know.

His father turned, zipping up his parka. "You stay right where you are, young man," he said sternly. "I don't want to lose both of you."

But Allie wasn't paying attention. "What's that?" he asked suddenly, pointing toward the outdoors. "Listen!"

His father stopped moving, stopped breathing. "What?" he asked after a second. "I don't hear anything."

Allie stood without moving. "There!" he said smiling. "There it is again."

For a moment more both stood motionless, straining to hear. A thin, high, rather frightened sound finally reached them through the chinks around the doors. Allie's father finally broke his trancelike silence and leaped out the door, standing at attention at the top level of the stairway there. Allie followed, only to be told "Quiet!" by his anxious father as Allie's boots galumphed on the wooden deck. Together they stood a moment more.

"Hey!" came a faint voice in the darkness at them. "Isn't *anybody* here?"

"Tessa!" shouted her father, jumping down the steps two at a time. "Tessa! Where are you? We're coming, Tessa!"

Allie's father was swallowed up in darkness. Allie waited atop the steps and then descended carefully, uncertain how exactly he should greet Tessa when he found her. It wasn't that he was disappointed. Not exactly. But the story he would have to tell the guys now came down to the same old thing, just another dumb thing done by someone else's dumb sister. You couldn't really call it spellbinding anymore, or even sort of exciting. Now it was just dumb.

His father and Tessa were standing entwined not more than thirty feet onto the snow in front of Allie as he approached.

"Are you all right, Tessa?" he heard his father ask worriedly. "You must be frozen. How could you get down alone, with the patrol out around you?"

"Patrol?" Tessa asked. "What are they doing?"

"Looking for you," answered her father. "We thought you'd been hurt somewhere and couldn't get help. Or had had an accident, a serious one. Tessa, I'm so glad you're all right!" Mr. O'Connell hugged Tessa again, and Allie, almost within visual range now, heard Tessa asked muffledly, as though she were talking through her father's parka. "But have you found Allie?"

"Allie?" said her father, puzzled.

"Of course, Allie," Tessa said rather impatiently. "What do you think I was doing up there all this time? I was looking for *that* little twerp."

"But, darling," answered Mr. O'Connell, "Allie's been with me for hours now. He wasn't lost. Is that what you thought?"

Allie crunched up and stood a few feet away from the pair. "Hi," he said simply.

"Where've you been?" Tessa shot out angrily at him. "Where'd you disappear to?"

"I didn't," Allie replied. "I'm right here. Always have been."

"Oh no, you don't," Tessa said hotly. "You snuck off somewhere, just before the last run. I know what you had in mind, you wretched little mugger!"

"Tessa, what are you talking about?" asked her father. "Believe me, sweetheart, Allie's been right alongside me almost all afternoon."

"Not when I last saw you, he wasn't," Tessa defended.

"I didn't make the last run with Dad," Allie said. "I

was tired. *I* know when to stop, even if some people don't."

"This all sounds like a terrible mix-up, if you ask me," said Mr. O'Connell. "Don't quarrel, kids, please. I'm just so glad, so relieved we're all standing here together, at last."

Allie was amazed. His father hugged Tessa still again and, although the light was poor and what moon there was was almost hidden above by clouds, Allie could have sworn his father's eyes had tears in them.

"I guess we'd better tell the ski patrol that all's well that ends well, hadn't we?" said Mr. O'Connell suddenly. "You two kids get to the car. I'll just push off and try to locate someone to tell the emergency's past."

Mr. O'Connell started to trot toward the north, toward the Eskimo/Prospector area, his boots scuffing and sliding in the crusted snow.

"Well, that's some dimwitted trick you pulled," Allie said as soon as his father was out of earshot.

"Let me tell you something, junior," Tessa answered. "Maybe I caused a little ruckus, but I sure as hell put a crimp in your hot plan."

"My plan?" asked Allie, genuinely astonished. "What are you talking about?"

"Don't play innocent with me, Allie O'Connell," said his sister, stepping out of her skis and hoisting them onto her shoulder. "You were going to torture Daddy and you know it."

"You're out of your bird."

"Don't you talk that way to me!"

"I can if I want to," Allie said. "Especially when it fits."

"You are beneath contempt!" said Tessa, starting to climb down from the snow onto the cement walkway, heading toward the darkened parking lot.

"Just tell me one thing," Allie said, following her,

dropping behind a second to grab his own skis and poles, "how did you get down without the patrol seeing you? Which trail did you take?"

"If you must know," Tessa said, "I made my own trail, thank you very much. And though you'd be the last person in the world to admit it, you should thank me for being so worried about you."

"Why?" Allie asked. "I wasn't in any trouble."

"One more word out of you and you will be," Tessa threatened.

"Big talk," Allie answered. "Bit talk from a crazy lady."

3.

I'm not an antisocial person. Also, I'm not bad-looking. I do have standards, of course, and regardless of my father's forever reminding me that there are as many worthwhile human beings in the world as there are (almost) human beings to begin with, I figure it's up to each of us to make up his or her mind and then stick with it until proven wrong. (Which hardly ever happens.) I mean, life is too short to spend a lot of time hanging around with questionable types, people who really don't amuse you or offer anything important. And if I don't make choices for myself, who will?

All this is to say that when Charlotte invited me to her party, I wasn't exactly thrilled. Not that there was any doubt I'd go. After all, Denver isn't the hottest place in the world to spend a Saturday night alone. As a matter of fact, it's not such a hot place to spend

Saturday night anyway. If you're lucky, you get invited out to a basketball game (which means sitting and cheering and trying not to get all sweated up—together an impossibility) by someone on the team, and then afterward you have to put up with all sorts of juvenile behavior. Like trying to force a beer down. (Which I think is about the palest drink in the world, and the silliest. I mean, if you wanted to get loaded, it would take an awful lot of beer to do the job and mostly all you'd end up doing would be making twenty or thirty trips to the john, which, by itself, isn't incredibly feminine.) Or, if you're luckier, maybe going to a movie like *Blazing Saddles* or *Summer of '42* (so you can laugh hysterically at that *one scene,* but also have to somehow pretend *you* don't know what that boy is in the drugstore to buy) or maybe *Billy Jack.*

The real dividing line, deciding whether to go out on Saturday or not, depends actually not so much on who asks you, but on how old they are. I mean, what is more humiliating than having your own parents (or his) have to drive you around town, drop you off, and then pick you up? And the absolutely embarrassing attempts some adults make at being friendly and "interested" (my father's word)!

Most of the time, if you want to know, I'd rather go somewhere with Charlotte alone, or maybe with another girl or two, and just hang around. In the summer, if we can swing it, sort of bum around Elitch's Gardens and pretend to be very world-weary and sophisticated, being whistled at by guys or flirting just a little, safe really because you know you're all together and nothing can happen to three of you at one time. Amusement parks aren't all that much fun, but you certainly do get to see what the populace looks like. Or maybe getting somehow to Roller City West, which is not only good exercise, but also means you get to tramp around in *very* tight jeans and a sweater that's at least one size too small. I, of course, don't really need to do that. I've plenty on top anyway, and accenting it, it seems to me, sometimes only makes girls who have less uneasy and envious and, ultimately, depressed. Hee-hee: it's not easy being a sex symbol! You can also hang out at the Alpine, if ice-skating is more your style. But mostly what you get over there is junior high school kids, and thank heavens that's all behind me now.

Wintertimes are a bit harder to fill, on weekends anyway. Unless you're going with someone, most of the time you spend indoors and at home, with "the girls." I don't have to tell you how depressing *that* is. Which is why, in the first place, I go skiing at all. I'm a natural athlete, sort of, and it's easy for me to do pretty well. More importantly, going away with Daddy or even with Allie and my mother means I can say, "I'm busy," and actually not be lying or making anything up. Or sometimes, when I feel "romantic" in a way most people don't understand, I'll just hole up in my room (such as it is now) and listen to KOAQ-FM, letting myself sink into the soft rock and imagining all sorts of things (which I see no need to admit here). These "withdrawals" (my mother's word) drive everyone bats, Allie and Mother, that is. My mother says she's only grateful I don't have my spells more often than once a month or so, because it drives her crazy to have me around half-dead and "mooning."

Anyway, I am not against people.

Charlotte's party was the first at-home of the basketball season. Which means she was going to have it downstairs, in her basement, and her parents were going to be upstairs, in the kitchen. Theoretically, having adults there as chaperons makes everyone else's parents happy, and without this, most kids couldn't get out. But mostly this applies to the girls. The guys couldn't care less. They figure that wherever it's dark it's open season, and you can't blame a man for trying. (If you want to know, I do.) Besides, some of the rougher guys always think they can intimidate someone's well-meaning parent. Which, on occasion, I've seen happen.

When Charlotte first told me about her plan, I wasn't too enthusiastic. Not that I don't like parties. It's just that being in an almost pitch-dark room, pretending to dance when all you're really doing is rubbing against each other, trying to avoid a straying hand or two, and somehow, through it all, making people believe you're having the time of your life, is no easy thing.

Especially when you consider Charlotte's guest list.

First of all, you have to remember the kind of girl Charlotte is: Game. O.K. Now, about three-quarters of the guys she's invited are also Game, which is to say they all belong to the Aufsteiger, which is this club we have at school for mountain climbers. Mountain climbers! There are about five girls in the club, too, though Charlotte didn't invite them wholesale, just rather selectively.

Now, you might think mountain climbers as a breed are, well, sort of perfect men. Quiet, strong, intense, agile, determined. Not very far even from the old "strong, silent type" you hear about on late movies. Wrong!

Some of them are. Maybe two: John Twiss and Fred Jacobson. But even these two change all the time. Twiss has a sneaky sense of humor and a very fast right hand (if you're not alerted in advance), and Jacobson is, under all the bravado (another trait that seems to belong to this group), really just boring.

The rest are guys just out for a good time, looking for something to do that doesn't involve girls and builds up their *machismo,* which means, loosely, "manhood," although as far as I'm concerned these guys have a long way to go. Beer-drinking and swearing and hollering and telling dirty jokes and getting hysterical over their own senses of humor is not the most interesting collection of habits to face in the dark. Most of these guys like to call themselves "animals," and I for one am not going to disagree. You might say they were as close to a professional mashers team as you can get.

Anyway, Charlotte invited them. Lord knows why, except that she keeps trying to prove to the world how gutsy she is and how much one of the guys she can be. I myself don't want to be one of the boys. I don't even want to be one of the girls. I just want to be me, whatever that turns out to be.

Another half-dozen guys were from the team, tall stringy types (I notice Charlotte did not invite any black players) or very short, muscular, speedy types. Out of all the above, there *was* one boy I did sort of think was cute. Which is why (apart from not having anything better to do) I went at all. There's an equality about me and Toby Bridgeman that I like, though he's probably not aware of it particularly.

First, we're about the same height, five-six. No one on the basketball team took Toby seriously when he first showed up for practice. He just grinned, took the floor, and ran circles around everybody else, which took care of *that*. No one really takes me seriously, either, which is O.K. because I haven't yet decided what it is I'm serious about.

We both have reddish-blond hair and blue eyes, although his are bluer than mine, mine being pale blue and rather close to being called "watery," which terrifies me.

He has a younger brother who's a pal of Allie's, which is both good and bad. Bad because I can't ever even mention Toby's name or it will get back to him; good because if I *do* ever want him to know I'm moderately interested in his welfare, he will.

And he's only fifteen and a half. Which means there is someone else in the world who can't drive, can't just jump in a car and pick up kids and head off into the night. Not that we both don't go along once in a while with other people who can. But, well, we're just somehow closer because we're closer to the ground, if you know what I mean.

I don't want to give the impression we're "going together" or anything like that. A lot of kids in our school do go together, and there is always intrigue and gossip and guessing about who and how far and where, and then, ultimately, why it all fell apart. That's not for Toby and me. Our "relationship," if you can call it that, is very subtle.

I mean we smile at each other, and once, at another of Charlotte's parties, we danced together for two entire records. Slow ones.

It's a start.

I realize I haven't said anything about what girls Charlotte invited. Well, really, that's not terribly interesting. I mean, girls are either people you like or you don't. You don't spend a lot of time (as you do with boys) trying to figure out why one might be a friend and another not. You just take a look, size up, and decide inwardly. And that's it. Not that you don't have some very good reasons. But these mostly you keep to yourself in the interest of being polite, and you keep nodding and smiling and saying "hello" as you walk a little more quickly down the hall, away from them. To be honest, one of the reasons you run is because some girls are just too beautiful; if you don't happen to think of yourself as pretty, the last thing in the world you want happening is some passing guy to stand and look and compare. I mean, sometimes even a sweet-looking, rather well-put-together person like me turns out, comparatively, a "dog." Not exactly ego-building.

Anyway, Charlotte *did* invite some girls. There's no point in listing them all, especially the ones who *are* going with someone because, just like married women, sooner or later they all end up echoing and agreeing with their hearts' desires, and you start thinking of them as a pair instead of individuals. Women's Lib has reached a lot of women, I'm sure, but it hasn't yet hit my particular age group. I suppose mostly because we're not a terrifically secure bunch of people to begin with, and I think Women's Lib really demands that you be secure before you open your mouth. You can see why it isn't going to work here.

So you have group one. The steadies. Group two, inevitably with Charlotte, are her pals from the Auf-steiger. Which is to say two or three equally competitive types who never worry about their figures or how much they eat or what they eat because they're all health freaks. Group three is rather different.

Charlotte feels that age makes no difference between friends. I can see, as we all grow older, that this might be so. But now, at this very minute, I think she's wrong. First of all, boy to girl, it's true that you get seniors seeing sophomores, a lot. But that's about the only case where her theory holds. Girls older than us, in eleventh or twelfth grades, are *very* conscious of who they are and with whom they're seen. Which is to say they don't really like to hang around with new-comers. They already have their cliques and their little gossip mills, and the amount of interest they have in us is about enough to fill a thimble—unless one of us invades their territory and *is* going out with an upper-classman.

Now, I am absolutely convinced I'm right about this. But just to screw me up, Charlotte always invites some older girls who always (to further complicate matters) show up. My theory is that they're interested in holding onto what they think is theirs. Charlotte's theory is that a party is a party and if it's fun, why not go?

Charlotte has another theory. That I'm so full of defense mechanisms I'm unable to see people clearly.

Of course I disagree, violently. I happen to think my
eyesight and my own values and reactions are true and
sharp. For example, in group three, there aren't a lot
of girls I like. Not because they're stuck-up and snotty.
Not because they stick together like soggy chocolate to
its wrapper. Not because they think they're superior
and think *we* are infants. Not because you have to
kowtow and bow and scrape if ever you want to get
into a club or something. But really because I think,
morally, they're—loose.

That's old-fashioned, I know. The very word,
"loose." But that's the way I feel and there's no getting
round it.

O.K. What exactly am I trying to say?

Simply this: I don't think it's fair or honest to lead
boys along, to tease them, to use them for (later) target
practice. Sure, we're all going to grow up and get married or have careers or whatever, and of course we
have to know how to operate in what is still mostly a
man's world. But I don't happen to think the process is
one we should be so eager to rush. I mean, being young
and having fresh ideals and hopes and ambitions is important to me. I'm not about to jump into a sort of
pseudosophisticated mirror-world where we're all practicing our wiles and sharpening our wits for the big
battles to come.

I have the feeling I'm still not being explicit. Take an
example. In the group of kids Charlotte likes to think
she's accepted by, older girls I mean, there are three or
four girls I know who, I think, are almost harlots. And
teases. And just asking for trouble.

It's one thing to sit in World History and watch Sybil
Gibson in the front row arranging her hair. "Arranging
her hair" means she sits there, her legs tucked up under her, and raises both arms to her head—stretching
an already two-sizes-too-small sweater against her
chest. It's quite a show, believe me, and every boy in

the room watches with the kind of attention every teacher in the world wishes he could command. Of course, with Sybil this really *is* playing. She's about five feet nine and weighs probably a hundred and thirty pounds. Besides, she has a sense of humor about herself, which helps. Yes, she's teasing, but also yes, the boy who wants to mess around with *her* had better be strong!

But it's quite another thing to watch, or rather *hear*, someone else in a dark corner in someone's rec room, or in the back row of the movies, or in a car, saying "No, don't," while letting the boy in question "do." And then cutting everything off.

Charlotte has explained over and over to me that girls who do this are really only taking pleasure in having desirable bodies, in learning how to use them, and mean no one any harm. Well, I for one object to making boys feel like idiots.

For example, three girls I know (all invited to Charlotte's) turn on like neon at the drop of a hat. They don't even seem to care that they've just finished making a wreck out of some poor sex-hungry boy before they swing around and send out their homing signals to someone else, sometimes even in the same room! Jennie Munson, Fran Stenner, and "O.K." McCall are the three I'm referring to, and in my own mind I call them "Macbeth's witches"—when shall those three meet again, in lightning, thunder, or in rain, to practice an art that drives men mad?

I'm not going to tell you how "O.K." got her nickname. You'd have to be insane not to understand!

"Banjo" Brown was humming away in the kitchen upstairs when we all piled into Charlotte's house. "Banjo" is Charlotte's father, so-called because he plays a you-know-what. Frequently, Mr. Brown starts plucking away at very opportune times, but more of this later.

The party got off to a good-enough start. Old East High had come through on its first outing of the season by a pretty considerable margin, and there was a lot of hand-slapping as each boy jumped down the final few steps into the rec room, shouting some kind of encouragement to his peers, who needed no encouragement at all. Why is it that the black "give-me-five" or whatever is suddenly such a neat trick to be able to do? I remember once at a party being introduced to someone who held his hand palm up, and when I took it to shake it politely, he nearly had a fit laughing. I mean, should a *girl* slap a boy's hand in greeting? Where are you, Emily Post? It occurs to me that Charlotte, naturally, being "game," would instantly understand and nearly throw her hand at someone else's.

At first, which is customary, the girls sort of hung together along one wall, waiting for the fellas to get whatever it is out of their systems and then to remember this was not a strictly stag evening. If you can believe it, a lot of the girls' whispering had to do with the boys' physiques, which baffles me, for one. I mean, if someone looks good, that's enough. But listening to Jeannie and Fran and Charlotte dissect each boy as he leapt into the room was pretty startling. Sometimes, even though they whispered, I heard words I've only ever seen and blushed at reading one of my mother's "modern" novels.

Pretty soon, though, things died down a bit, and the girls who were going steady wound up standing with their boys, arm in arm, sometimes stroking a back or the back of a neck possessively, which I think is absolutely sickening. I mean, that went out with all the movies where the female stars were dressed by Edith Head and always had a dance scene followed by fireworks—you know what I mean, where the camera pans away from a passionate embrace up into the sky outside the window and you're supposed to imagine what is happening while the Roman candles explode.

Somebody started the stereo. Toby Bridgeman was nowhere in sight, even though I thought he'd hit the rec room floor at the same time as Mike Prince, Charlotte's pick of the litter. With thirty or so kids milling around in semidarkness, you wouldn't think finding just one would be such a trial, but it was. Finally, though I'm much too polite to tell you from where he came, Toby materialized and smiled at me across the room. I smiled back, but didn't move. It's not feminine to be too eager, although I'm berserk for those scenes in movies where the Confederate soldier comes limping home and his hard-working, half-starved wife looks up from hanging something on a line and sees him, and they run at each other (in slow motion, of course) and have this incredible wild reunion scene. Anyway, Toby and I smiled at each other, and sort of nodded, and he started to weave his way through the crowd toward my side of the room, when—naturally!—Charlotte's mother (Mary Lou) marched down the stairs into the rec room and stepped right in front of Toby. She was carrying food and wearing a big grin, and joked teasingly as she edged around one clutching couple after another, heading toward a sideboard against which I was leaning.

Naturally, being well-bred, I turned away from Toby and offered to help Mrs. Brown set out the stuff. "Banjo" appeared at the stairway, carting a huge tray of soda and diet stuff to drink, and stopped on his way across the room to congratulate team members and to tease Charlotte about status-seeking, entertaining only winning teams and so forth.

The appearance of adults set the party back a level, as it does every time. Not that the food wasn't good. I mean, ever since the U.S. government came out saying pizza was nourishing and good for you, there's been a sanction on junk food which everyone loves. What I mean is that offering food to high school boys is calculated to divert their attention from other, perhaps more worthwhile pursuits.

Which of course happened. The room was divided all over again as the guys attacked the sideboard as though they were prisoners of war. The girls stood around. One or two were lucky enough to be remembered and to have slices handed back to them. The rest of us just stood by patiently, watching and waiting, and then, finally, daintily wolfing down what was left.

The Browns, as custom demands, had withdrawn again to the kitchen upstairs, and the stereo was turned up and the lights were turned down. Life, for about half an hour, was splendiferous.

Even though I basically disagree and feel uncomfortable, there's an exciting kind of tension dancing publicly with a boy you like. Half of his attention is centered on you (which is good), and half is centered on being seen by his friends (which is bad). What this means is that sometimes Toby got very tender and sweet and held me very close, and sometimes (because I guess he felt he had to) he tried to be what my mother calls "fresh."

This sort of puts us girls in a difficult position. I mean, you don't want to embarrass the boy and scream, "Hands off, you klutz!" He'd die of embarrassment, and you'd be without a date for the next six months. On the other hand, you can't afford to let him think he can take liberties. After all, a girl is a human being, too, and is just as important and private as a boy, and deserves some sort of real courtesy, even if what the boy is always thinking about has nothing at all to do with manners.

I'm not talking about the girls who are going steady. Their problem, if they care, is how to keep their boy, or keep him out of the hands of another girl. Our problem (us unattached ladies, that is) is how to get a boy in the first place. This is much more nervous-making and has far fewer rules and regulations to follow.

I read somewhere, maybe in *Cosmopolitan,* that a boy's peak sexual years are his teens, about sixteen maybe, and that a woman's best time is in her thirties. This alone should explain some of our problems; they're all hot to trot, and we're only mildly interested. Terrific.

Anyway, for a while the room looked just like any other teen-age groping and grappling session, figures swaying rhythmically to a lot of very loud rock music (almost ignoring the beat of the music, because who wants to dance apart when you can dance up close?) and lots of snuffling (which I call those sounds you hear and are curious about but can't identify) and giggling, and everyone bumping into each other every so often and almost seeming to be held upright by the other bodies around them.

Little did I know, or think, that the sound of a Fresca being popped open sounds almost exactly like a can of Coors being popped open. Or that the little knots of people in darker corners, passing what at a distance looked like Diet Pepsi around, were really formed around whoever in the group had a bottle and was generously dropping a little bourbon or vodka into the aluminum cans.

Now, I have to say, in Toby's defense, that I really don't think he *wanted* to imitate the other guys. There's a thing called "peer pressure" we're always reading about, and Toby seems much too sensible to me to let that get to him. Still, when Tommy Andersen cut in on us (I admit to being surprised) and when Toby backed away very politely and said "Thank you, Tessa" (which just goes to show you what kind of really thoughtful person he is), it never occurred to me that he'd head for a corner and hit the bottle.

Actually, I had other things to think about. Tommy Andersen is about six feet two inches tall, and for starters that can throw a girl off her stride. Within seconds I could feel my calves begin to ache, and I could hear my breath coming just a little shorter and shallower than ordinarily. Also, I wasn't exactly sure whether I was supposed to make conversation and try to be "interested," or whether I should just hang on and let Tommy hum in my ear, all the while signaling the nerves around my waist and "lower waist" to be alert. As for the solution to this question, I really had little to do with finding it. Tommy wrapped himself around me (he'd never in his life before shown even the slightest interest in me) and asked, "Having fun?" When I said yes, that seemed enough for him and his arms pulled me closer in and it suddenly occurred to me that the sounds of my breathing could (if Mother's trashy novels were accurate) be described as "fast, throbbing, eager." I tried to hold my breath then, and just every so often, out of the corner of my mouth, I gulped a silent swallow of life-giving oxygen.

When Toby cut back in, I need hardly report I was (momentarily) relieved. And happy. I remember looking around and sort of having the feeling that the crowd had thinned out some. I didn't try to squint through the darkness to see if people were necking on couches or not, because I just assumed that. I also remember hearing "Banjo" Brown singing away upstairs in the kitchen, and I heard a few people up there clapping hands in time to his song, but it did *not* occur to me that the kids who had staggered up the steps and out of the sort of dingy, tense, sweaty world below had made an escape to safety.

It should have. Toby smiled a silly sort of grin at me, which even in the dark I could see was unusual, and opened his arms. I was happy enough to forget about being ladylike and just sort of naturally glided into them, which was a super feeling, I have to tell you. But then everything sort of dissolved, if you know what I mean.

Toby gripped me pretty hard and whispered into my left ear, "Feeling O.K.?"

Unsuspecting, I said, "Super."

Then he said, "I just bet!"

Do I have to give you a blow-by-blow of what followed? Let's just say that Toby Bridgeman's left hand didn't seem to know what his right hand was supposed to be doing, or vice versa.

"Toby, stop," I said, whispering.

"Oh, Tessa," he said, sort of speaking very slowly and in a kind of slurry trance, "you know how much I like you."

I didn't exactly feel this was the time to find out how much he liked me, and I said so.

Toby started to protest that he was only human and that I was so incredibly "desirable" (which really blew my mind, if you want to know), when all hell broke loose in a corner across the room.

It was almost as though the sound effects had gotten mixed up in a film. The first thing I remember hearing was a crash of broken glass. And *then* a slap, a really loud *crack!* across someone's face (I assumed). And then, finally, "O.K." McCall's voice shrieking out into the darkness around us all: "I *told* you, creep, to cut that out!"

There was some sort of mumbling, and then "O.K." again: "Who do you think I am, for God's sakes? Or should I say, *what* do you think I am? Whatever it is, buster, you're dead wrong!"

I was absolutely cemented to the floor. I mean, "O.K." has a normal voice which is rather nice, soft and musical, and this girl somewhere out there in the darkness sounded as though she were at least forty and had led a life that could best be described as "difficult." I mean it was really scary. Of course, "O.K." *is* two years older than I am, but still.

Anyway, thank goodness no one put on the lights, because just then I heard Jennie Munson say, "What is this, anyway? Open season? Is there some sort of secret society at work here?"

Tommy Andersen: "For Pete's sake, Jennie, let it go."

"No," Jennie said. "I don't think I should. You guys seem to think we're all just dying to reward your slobbering all over us. Well, think again!"

I can't tell you how odd this all was, especially in the dark. Another voice (I couldn't tell whose) snaked out: "Come off it, 'O.K.' It's not the first time."

Toby turned to me as another terrific whack rang out. "Let's hit the kitchen," he said.

I didn't even nod. I just grabbed his hand and pulled him through the crowd. Behind us, "O.K." started to cry. "I'm getting out of here," she said.

A light was turned on as we had almost reached the top of the stairs, but neither one of us looked back.

Coming upstairs and walking into the kitchen was like entering another world. "Banjo" Brown was seated on a sink-counter, his gold-plated banjo in his lap, strumming away, and everyone there (there must have been a dozen people besides Charlotte's mother) was singing along to "Hello, Dolly."

People made room for us on one of the picnic benches that the Browns use for family feeding, and we sat down, not even daring to look at each other.

I didn't start to sing along right away. I was still almost in shock. I just looked at the room and the people and tried to breathe quietly.

You could still hear the Stones from downstairs, and the volume was such that the beat of their music rose up from the floor into the soles of your feet and fought against the music that Mr. Brown played.

The room itself wasn't full. It's huge, to begin with, and very yellow and white with lots of antique pewter standing all over. There are cabinets of walnut on each wall, and everything is built-in: dishwasher, refrigerator, stove, grills, ovens. The curtains are a print of Johnny Appleseed and very cheerful, and there's a sort of Tiffany light above the center of the room that makes things colored and rosy and comforting.

I could hear footsteps on the basement stairs, but no one more came into the room right away. I figured that "O.K." and Jennie and maybe a few others were on their way out and home, maybe saying goodbye and thanks (for *that?*) to Charlotte. After a few minutes, when we both felt better, I heard Toby begin to sing very quietly along with the crowd in the kitchen. Mr. Brown was into a medley, ages old, of course: "Harvest Moon," "For Me and My Gal," and "Moonlight Bay." Toby began to sort of sway with everyone else in the room, back and forth, and I looked over as his shoulder nudged mine and he smiled, sort of sheepishly, and I forgave him everything downstairs. He took my hand and nodded a little, urging me I guess to sing along too, and so I did.

Charlotte and Mike Prince and Tommy and whoever was left downstairs pretty soon gave up whatever was still happening there and started, a couple at a time, to emerge, standing first in the doorway to the kitchen, and then, as "Banjo" looked up and grinned at them, coming in and sitting or kneeling or leaning wherever they could and joining the songfest. (I need hardly report that old camp songs were not far away, "Long, Long Trail" and "Tell Me Why" surfacing and being subjected to some of the wildest harmonies you've ever imagined.)

I'll tell you: sometimes a parent like "Banjo" can

make it seem as though the really wretched time you've had never existed. Which is no small talent.

Charlotte was a pretty lucky girl to have a full-time father, I thought.

4.

Tessa would have seen her father's car sooner but for the wind. A brutally icy breeze was directed, oddly, from the south straight up Ash Street and into Tessa's face as she walked homeward from the bus stop on Colorado Avenue. Her head was ducked and pulled down into her collar, and her arms, which carried books and note papers and her purse, were crossed protectively in front of her as she leaned into the wind and counted her hurried footsteps on the sidewalk.

She had already turned right and started up her short driveway toward the stairway that led to their apartment when she stopped, suddenly, and turned. She couldn't see what it was she thought she'd seen as she sped toward warmth and hot chocolate upstairs, and so she had to retrace her steps a bit and then stop, peering around the corner of the neat white house. It *was* there, her father's car, a battered and bruised Mercedes sedan. Seeing it made Tessa smile, for the car had been but another wedged crumb in her mother's throat. "If you can't afford to have it repaired, you can't afford to drive it," she had told her (then) husband. His reply: "I could afford to do both if you only had the slightest idea of how and where to spend what little we have." This had led to a stand-off line: "You only keep that for status, Richard, and you know it."

There was an afterthought in her mother's mind: "Like us."

Tessa hugged herself and moved back into the shelter of the side of the house. An idea crossed her awareness, but she batted it away as childish and naive. People just don't get together again, no matter how good it would be for either of them, not after they've taken those final steps to freedom. Besides, looking at life as an adult (which Tessa felt entitled to do), it was clear that separation had been devoutly wished by both her parents. The actual deed may have been wrenching, but, like a band-aid pulled off suddenly, most of the pain was in the movement and not real or lasting.

Well, what could she do? She didn't want to interrupt, but she *was* turning to a pillar of ice standing where she was.

Why was her father there at all at that odd time of day?

No matter what his reason, no matter what he came to say, he had clearly arrived before either she or Allie was scheduled to return from school. Whatever was on his mind was something meant for her mother alone, then.

(Another secret thought flashed across Tessa's mind: suppose she was wrong, suppose right that very minute, upstairs, her mother and father were together reunited, making new and unbreakable vows?)

She shivered. One thing: if she stayed hidden outdoors, somewhere out of sight but within close enough distance to observe her father's leaving, at least she could warn Allie not to go barreling upstairs when *he* got home. Actually, she would be doing a good deed, if she did that.

But a surprising and strong gust of wind broke around the side of 2341 Ash Street and sent her almost running for her own entryway. She reached out a hand to the doorknob, grasped it, and stopped. There was enough room, if she were terribly quiet and careful, to simply slip inside the door and huddle at the bottom of the stairs there, one hand on the doorknob behind her for a speedy escape. That way she could warn Allie *and* keep warm.

She looked back at the driveway and saw a swirl of fallen leaves begin to whip in a whirlwind and climb from the pavement toward her eyes. Holding her breath, she pulled open the door and inched her way into the house, stopping as soon as the door closed shut behind her with what she thought was an intentionally ruthless and loud "snap!"

At first she was only aware of her parents' voices, somewhere above her, reasonably remembered as a hum in childhood on dark nights when she and Allie had been put to bed. She leaned against the door and stifled a huge relieved sigh, a gratifying signal of comfort found once again, a haven from the Colorado wind.

She decided that she didn't dare put down her books or purse in case she might have to flee quickly; she had the image of herself flailing about in the doorway, trying to catch sailing texts as they seemed gravity-drawn back again to the floor out of her reach. She did allow herself to take one tentative and very silent pace away from the door toward the first level step ahead of her. She might actually hear something interesting, and besides, with her hand always on the knob behind her, her retreat was safely guarded and easily attained.

The voices of her parents began to clear in her awareness and single words, first, and then brief phrases were intelligible.

". . . what the rush is," her mother said.

Her father's first words couldn't be heard clearly. Then: ". . . besides it's what we want."

"You or Zandra?"

Tessa heard her father's footsteps pace above her. She couldn't hear any further explanation. He must have stepped away from her mother, toward a wall or maybe facing the kitchen, which absorbed his words.

"And why couldn't it be after Christmas?" she heard her mother ask plainly. "The holiday will be bad enough, Richard, as it is. After all, it *is* the first Christmas we've all been apart."

". . . told you," answered her father.

"Don't you think some small consideration is due your own children? Zandra's a big girl, I assume."

"We just think that Christmas is a festive season, Dorie, and this might even make the whole thing easier for the kids. Just one more big, fun party."

"Which I assume Zandra is paying for?"

"Don't. I didn't come here to argue."

"I'm sorry," Tessa's mother said, lowering her voice. Tessa heard a glass being set on a table and then her mother's footsteps, although her direction wasn't traceable. You could always tell when someone moved in the apartment because, though the house *seemed* sturdy and solid, it literally shook from the changing pressure and shifting weights of its occupants.

". . . more than you did me?" asked her mother, very quietly. Timidly, it seemed to Tessa below.

"Don't, Dorie. It's just all—it's all different now. You can't compare these things."

"I'm trying not to, but I can't help it. Is she prettier, too?"

Tessa closed her eyes and bit her lower lip. *Please, please!* she prayed. *Don't let him tell her she's already seen her!*

"For God's sakes, Dorie, are you going to martyrize yourself over this, too? You're an attractive, intelligent woman. Your life isn't over."

"Well, a part of it certainly is!" Tessa's mother answered angrily. "When out of nowhere, a man I've lived with and given children to walks in and without warning announces he's leaving!"

"If I hadn't, you would have, sooner or later," said Mr. O'Connell. "We both know what was happening underneath, the frustrations, the cover-ups."

"*I* had nothing to cover up!"

"Listen, Dorie, I'm not here to rehash the whole thing. I only came over to see you without the kids hanging around, so I could tell you myself, face to face, and spare you the pain, or the embarrassment, of reading about it all somewhere, or hearing it from one of your ever-well-meaning friends."

"Leave my friends out of this!"

"That's exactly what I'm trying to do!"

There was a silence above Tessa, and she let out her breath. When her father spoke again, he was calmer.

"Look, Dorie, I know this is painful. Not just for you, I understand that, but for the kids, as well. You can help them, you know. We both can. We can make it all into an adventure, into something they'll understand and be comfortable in. Zandra and I aren't in competition with you, you know. You've done a damn fine job with both Allie and Tessa. If anything, we just hope to be able to enjoy them every so often as the really great people they're becoming."

"You think it will be easy for them?"

"I think we can both help make it less difficult, if we want to. If you want to."

"Why is it always me?" Dorie O'Connell suddenly shouted. "Why is it always something *I* have to be careful about?"

"Dorie, I'm not criticizing you. I'm only—"

"Oh, yes, you are! Beneath all this is exactly that! And I'm not going to take it anymore, not all on myself. If you want to tell Tessa and Allie, *you* tell them! *You* make it easy for them!"

"Look, that's fine with me," said Tessa's father. "I'll be glad to do that. All I'm saying is that you could back me up for once and be supportive, for God's sakes, instead of always undermining and sniping!"

"What?"

"Now, take it easy," Mr. O'Connell said. "I didn't really mean that. It just slipped out."

"Freudianly, I suppose," said her mother bitterly.

Her father cleared his throat. "Listen, Dorie, the kids are O.K. I think they've taken this all with really good grace. Maybe Allie's a little more comfortable with it than Tessa, but that's only natural. She's at an age, I guess, where everything is a little more dramatic and tragic than it deserves to be. But, really, so far they've come through just as *we* have. I'm only interested in maintaining that even keel, Dorie. That's all. It's something we both owe the kids."

A crash of glass sounded upstairs. Tessa gasped and gripped the doorknob behind her more tightly. "How dare you!" her mother shouted. "Don't you dare talk about owing the kids *anything!* What about me? What do you owe *me?*"

Mr. O'Connell's footsteps were quick ones. Tessa thought she could even hear the rustle of wool. "I'm getting out of here," her father announced. "If you ever calm down enough to think straight, call me."

"Oh, no, you don't!" Dorie O'Connell called out. "Don't think you can just walk away from this responsibility, too!"

"Dorie, I'm not walking. I'm only asking you to share it."

Tessa's hand seemed to close on the knob of its own decision. Within a few clandestine seconds, she was standing outside her door, seeing her own breath emerge into the late-afternoon shadows but not moving more than a step at a time, dazed. She didn't even hear Allie's racing hoofbeats on the driveway pavement.

"Hey, Dad's here!" Allie shouted as he ran full tilt toward Tessa. "What'd he bring you?"

Tessa started, as though aware and tolerant of Allie, but not really caring whether he was answered or considered or even existed. "Don't go in, Allie," she said evenly, without expression.

"Why not? He's my father, too."

"They're fighting."

Allie had not let Tessa's command stop his homeward progress. This announcement did. He turned and looked a moment at his sister. "Then why," he said finally, after thinking his statement through in advance, "are you standing out here?"

"What?" Tessa asked in return, not understanding.

"Let's go in and stop it," Allie suggested reasonably. "Why let them hurt each other any more?" He paused a moment, as though waiting for Tessa to agree and accompany him. When she didn't move, he grew impatient.

"Tessa, come on!"

Almost in a dream, Tessa nodded and started back toward the doorway to their upstairs apartment. Allie held the door open for her, and as she passed, he whispered at her, his blue-green eyes alight, "After all, Teresa. We are *responsible.*"

5.

This is *not* a bulletin. Everybody has to have a secret place. Sometimes it's inside yourself, sometimes outside. But it's real and private and important, even though you may not really understand why.

So it will come as no surprise that even I have a secret place. The Denver Art Museum.

That sounds esoteric (yet another favorite word), but it isn't, not really. A lot of people, I imagine, like museums and libraries and big quiet buildings in which they can lose themselves.

I don't mean anything supernatural or mystic or cultish. I mean where the outside thing—a room, some music, a picture—allows you to stop being who you really are and frees your imagination so you become, even for a minute, someone or something else.

From the outside, the museum certainly doesn't look like it could help you fantasize. I mean, it's a very solid-looking pile of stone. I guess the architects wanted to present an image of permanence rather than light. There are breaches and oddly shaped openings and windows all over, but your main impression is almost of a medieval battlement, the kind where there were slits in the stones so archers could fire out and down from their high perches.

Anyway, the building is impressive. It's seven or eight stories high and it looks positively impenetrable. Even when you walk in, your imagination hardly soars. Straight ahead of a sort of tunnel through which you enter is a large, supposedly informal lounge, where you can also get coffee and sandwiches and so forth from a cafeteria. The ceiling is about two stories tall, but still the room itself is furnished in what I call hospital modern. It has modular chairs, some covered in blue, others in purple, which sit on a brown tile floor, and there are columns of lights that shoot upward and reflect brightly the stainless steel fixtures themselves. Not that all this isn't comfortable when you've been hiking mile after mile through the galleries. But it certainly can't be called "tasteful," not in my mind, anyway. But this isn't what matters in a museum, is it? It's what's inside, what's in the collections, what's here to see and study and feel for.

Because that *is* what really counts, as far as I'm con-

cerned, in art. Responding. There's not a lot I like more
than seeing a canvas across a room and being suddenly
aware that I feel something for it. Or against it. It
makes me feel alive. It makes me feel as though the
artist has, negatively or positively, really got to his audience.

And that's, after all, all I am. I mean I can't paint
or draw or sculpt. But boy! can I *feel!*

What I'm trying to say here is that I'm about the
easiest pushover there is when someone asks me to react to something. I really react. I don't always talk
about it. Sometimes, even though I might want to, what
I feel I can't explain. Still, as that old saying goes, I
can tell you what I like most times, and if I'm lucky,
why.

But I can't when I try to describe my secret place.
All I can say is that I have a room in the museum
I return to whenever some instinct tells me it's time.
And that I have a piece of art in that same room that
wipes me out, that really makes the rest of the world
disappear when I'm looking at it, that makes me blind,
in a way, deaf, and dumb to almost anything else happening around me.

I stumbled on all this accidentally one afternoon last
winter. Our class had already visited the museum, on
a get-acquainted kind of field trip, but then, I guess,
we all were more interested in just getting away from
school than in actually seeing anything or learning anything. (That is only natural. I'm not apologizing for
it.)

But one afternoon last year, I had had to come
downtown to see if the main library had anything on an
English poet named Gerard Manley Hopkins (who's
a word painter more than a writer, as far as I'm concerned) that I could use in a report. At the best of
times, the library is a warm hangout for kids. At the
worst, it's calculated to make you feel incredibly guilty

because you're only there to get one thing and all around you are things you *know* you should care for and you don't. Anyway, I had found a few little items I could camouflage for my report and present in such a way that it seemed I'd been working on the thing for positively months, and there wasn't anything else I really wanted to do. Daddy was supposed to pick me up at five o'clock, on his way home, and I had an hour to kill. If I were being purposely titillating (I love that word!), I could say, I suppose, that something gothic and grim drew me from the library and across the parkway to the mysterious gray castle.

The truth was, I wasn't looking for anything in particular. I just wanted a change of scene.

I skipped the cafeteria in the lobby because, while I *was* starving, I was also at my best weight and there's no sense tempting fate. I shivered a little as I entered the building, glad to be free of the cold and wind, and shuffled my way almost aimlessly into an empty elevator and, by chance, punched the floor-button marked "3."

The third-floor gallery was not crowded. (I've never seen any of the galleries crowded; sometimes you can hear an elementary school class on a tour somewhere behind you, or in another room, but when they've passed and moved on, it hardly seems as though there were enough little kids involved to even call their gang a group.) I didn't even really pick the path I would follow. I just walked out of the elevator, and took a turn (I can't now remember which direction), and opened my eyes. For the first time.

I know this sounds stupid, especially if you're not as inexperienced as I am, but that afternoon, in the wintery shadows, Art hit Me. I'd seen things before: reproductions, prints, little pieces of Eskimo sculpture which is icy but somehow, because of the stone used, I guess, gets instantaneously warm when you hold it.

I'd seen works by van Gogh and Rubens and Sargent and Cézanne. I'd even sort of examined a Rembrandt once, and I can recognize a piece by Henry Moore pretty fast.

But there, in the third-floor gallery that held art of our own hemisphere, no kidding I went blind with joy and wonder. It was the first time, I think, that I'd ever known that really juicy things were done by natives of Colombia and Mexico and Peru. I don't mean ceramics and weavings and what I think is called pre-Columbian art. I mean paintings and drawings that are positively European-looking.

This is very hard for me to explain. What I'm trying to say is that Central and South American artists, in say the eighteenth and nineteenth centuries, were doing their own versions of what had already been done in Europe years before. Lots of landscapes and flower pictures (still lifes, I think), heroic scenes and pictures of legendary beings, gods and goddesses, and portraits and country vistas. The amazing thing is that, to me anyway, all these pictures really *did* almost look like the real things. (I just *know* that two hundred bodies have wheeled and spun in their graves, but really, the artists I'm talking about were amateurs, or so it seems to me. They were *copying*. They were painting in the "style of," trying to please their patrons by furnishing them with their own, less expensive, less valuable work that was purposely made to look as though it had been carried on shipboard from one continent to the other. Maybe this isn't fair, but that's the way it seems to me.)

Enough. What I'm saying is that for the first time in my life I realized that people who lived not very far away were working hard and producing and I'd never before seen any of their efforts.

I wandered around in a daze, every once in a while (after a quick look over my shoulder) *touching* a canvas to feel the thickness of the paint, or the texture,

r to follow a particular line across the surface of the
ainting, every few steps stopping to feel the heavy
old skin of even the pictures' frames.

Without being aware, I was drifting away from the
European kind of American painting and edging more
nd more closely into something else. I remember
watching my own hand leave the corners of a frame
hat was curlicued and carved and then lower to settle
on a kind of adobe-cement barrier, a low wall that ran
or about twenty feet or so and led me right into the
enter of a different kind of collection altogether.

I looked around and ahead I saw two enormous,
uge, heavy stone carvings: two heads of some sort of
ymbolic serpent. I blinked. I'd left all the fanciness and
ome straight into something simpler, almost scary.

I didn't like where I was, and without particularly
lanning to, I ducked into a room on my left.

Terrific! I run from intimidating stone snakes straight
nto a shadowy pale room where the first thing that
atches my eye is a figure of Death!

I mean, there is no mistaking that lady on that cart.
Her legs are bleached and almost thin enough to see
hrough; her skeletal hands carry a tiny bow and ar-
ow, with the bowstring already pulled to an almost
eady position. And the skull is smiling!

I looked up and for the first time saw the room in
which I stood. I was surrounded by adobe walls. A low,
ow ceiling. Candles and marks of devotion. Then I
nderstood. I was in a replica, a small, perfect copy of
ome sort of chapel or church.

It wasn't that this discovery took a lot of smarts. To
ny left, above me and behind glass, was the figure of
a thin, painted, bleeding Christ, his eyes closed and
ast down, his body taut on the Cross, a crown of
horns atop his sagging head.

But the miraculous thing was the sudden feeling I
got of peace from this figure. Of course, on his body

were painted the stigmata, and the bruises and cu‚
and running sores. But the face, the posture of th‚
head, the eyes painted in a dirtied, bloodied face—a‚
this was more resigned and final, and *expected,* tha‚
I'd ever before seen.

I think, for the first time, I was seeing something tha‚
sent out waves of love and peace and devotion. I'v‚
seen other artists' ideas of this—some pastoral, som‚
brutal. But this was the first figure I'd ever encoun‚
tered where Christ was *human.* And as human, *real.*

I don't know how long I stared up at him before ‚
finally looked for the little card that could tell m‚
something about the art itself. It wasn't enormousl‚
helpful or informative. All it said was that this was ‚
Crucifixion (thanks), carved wood bulto, gesso cov‚
ered and painted, early nineteenth century from Mora‚
New Mexico. It was also sixty inches tall.

I didn't then know what a bulto was, nor how on‚
covered whatever it was with gesso, whatever *that* was‚

I walked slowly backward, drifting again toward th‚
death cart.

Death Cart (*La Carreta de la Muerte*)

The Death Cart is drawn in the Penitente processions on a simulated journey to Calvary during Holy Week nights. The seated figure of Death
in the form of a skeleton with hollow eyes and
leering grin represents to the Penitentes the tri-
umph of death after the Crucifixion and before
the Resurrection. It was considered good luck to
be brushed by the cart during the procession. In
New Mexico, Death is a female known as La
Dona Sebastiana. As Death rides her cart she
holds a bow and arrow—a traditional Penitente
variation of the European interpretation of Death
as the reaper carrying a scythe.

"It was considered good luck to be brushed by the cart during the procession." Are you kidding? Like it used to be considered good luck to touch the shoulder of a hunchbacked person in the Middle Ages. I'd faint dead, if I had to do either!

I heard someone behind me and moved back a little so that whoever was there could step forward to read and see better if he wished. And I don't even know to this day whether the person there was a man or woman. I had stepped back and for some reason turned my head to the right and then, unconsciously, I was transfixed. I saw still another figure, but this one sent out signals of sadness, or grief. (Maybe you've run across the cliché, "ineffable grief." This means, according to my dictionary, beyond expression, indescribable. That's what leapt into my mind.)

As in a dream I moved toward a glass case and stared into it. I don't know whether I read the notation first or after or maybe somehow at the same time, but what I was gazing at was the figure of a youngish woman dressed mostly in red, holding a cruciform in her hands at chest level, looking up and into the distance.

Our Lady of Sorrows (Nuestra Señora de los Dolores)

Head and torso of carved cottonwood root, gessoed and painted, supported on hollow frame construction. New Mexico. Gift of the May D & F Company.

Was this Mary, then? Or just a figure of a woman during Christ's walk, seeing him laden and burdened and bleeding and thirsty, a man to be pitied and helped—a silent witness, rooted in grief and sorrow, immobile and awestruck?

And I began to have a feeling that this was not a woman at all, but a young girl, perhaps someone who

was just my own age. Surely at that moment in history
there were young people, too? People who saw and
believed, or who watched and scoffed. Momentarily I
tried to think of ever reading about someone like that,
someone like me back then who *was* involved or on the
scene. I hadn't.

I moved my face to the edge of the nonreflective
glass to study her. It was impossible not to feel her
youth, but her face was cracked, weathered, dry as
leather forgotten and unoiled. She was dressed, oddly I
thought, in red. She wore a red circular skirt to which, at
its bottom, was attached real lace. There was a white
apron around her waist, and a white cloth belt of some
kind. Her blouse was red, and she wore a white bib and
a funny kind of bow tie. Her cruciform was made of
brown beads and she clasped it devoutly in front of
her.

Her hair was brown, and I couldn't tell whether it was
dyed wool or flax or whether it actually might be
strands from a living person's head. Her mouth was
half open and her teeth looked more real than my own.
In the cracked, lined face were set two beautiful green-
black sightless eyes, raised to the distance somewhere,
seeing or imagining something that made her want to
weep, and beneath these *might* have been painted tears.
I couldn't tell.

I don't want to make too much of all this. Out of
what I felt, I mean, looking at her. After all, it was still
weeks or months before Mother and Daddy decided to
split up. And I wasn't in any kind of grand funk that
I can remember.

But she got to me.

I felt weak and saddened and oddly happy all at the
same time. My eyes sort of clouded over and I got a
funny prickling sensation from my ears down my neck
to my shoulders, the way I do when I hear some really
wonderfully romantic music. Even the light in the little

chapel seemed somehow brighter, thinner, as though she and I were on an incredibly high peak somewhere but not somewhere cold.

I knew that if I ever returned (and I also knew instantly that I would), I could almost communicate with this beautiful, fragile figure. That I could understand why she might be weeping. That, in a way, she and I could weep together and share joy. That we knew almost nothing of life, really, but we *sensed* a good deal about it; instinctively we both knew that tragedy walked hand-in-hand with happiness and that we alone would be to blame if Life was allowed to give us more of the first than the second.

I shivered a little as I stared at her.

I had done more than find my own secret place. I had found someone already there in it, someone—to love.

6.

She hadn't been able to stop talking. As though Tessa were starring in her own technicolor dream, starring in it and watching herself perform at the same time, she seemed to have lost control.

She, Allie, and their father were Sunday brunching at the Brown Palace Hotel. It had been Mr. O'Connell's idea, since the day was to be devoted to meeting and learning about the "Unsinkable" Mrs. Brown anyway, although Mr. O'Connell had been unable to discover whether Mrs. Brown or her husband, "J.J.," had ever had anything to do with the hotel itself, other than staying in it each time their house was redecorated.

From the first moments of being awake, Tessa had been conscious of a feeling in the pit of her stomach that obstinately refused to be identified as hunger or nerves. In Tessa's stomach the feelings were identical, and since she couldn't uncover either's reality, she didn't know whether to eat something or to ask her mother for (or not ask, just pocket) one of her tranquilizers. Knowing that they would eat heartily soon, Tessa simply put more sugar and milk into her morning tea and hoped.

At the hotel, after Mr. O'Connell had called for them and driven through a cloudy, threatening day downtown, Tessa had ordered an omelet. Her father had suggested that, just for fun, both she and Allie might like a morning "pick-me-up," a Bloody Mary. Allie's nose had wrinkled in disdain and distaste, but Tessa had accepted. After all, she had reasoned, since she felt adult, there was no reason not to behave as one.

But then she had begun to talk. Endlessly. Pointlessly. Maddeningly. As though the sound of her voice would bar anyone's intrusion or the inclusion of news or suggestions that could cause her distress.

Her father had listened with what Tessa realized was extraordinary patience. He had nodded and "uh-huhed" and asked questions that only served to push Tessa further into her monologue, that made her reflect tangentially from one scatterbrained topic onto another.

Allie simply stared at her during the meal and, from time to time, shook his head wonderingly.

When she found a piece of shell in her omelet, not eggshell but rather more like a piece of something that *lived* in a shell, like a crab, Tessa was only momentarily brought to a halt before rushing into what she knew inwardly was a totally uninformed tirade about hotel kitchens and food. When her father suggested they call the waitress over and send the omelet back to the kitchen, graciously and breathlessly Tessa demurred, saying after all what could one expect in Denver.

On the way to the car afterward, her father had put an arm around Tessa's shoulder and asked solicitously, "Honey, is there something troubling you? Something on your mind?"

Tessa had laughed, maturely she thought. "Gracious, no! Whatever makes you think that?"

Her father smiled and shook his head in puzzlement. "Well, it's just that I've never heard you go on so before. I never knew my daughter was such a vivid conversationalist."

Tessa then had forced herself to laugh, too. "I was only trying to make the meal amusing," she announced. "I mean, with the food in that place, I should think you'd be glad to have something else to think about."

Mr. O'Connell smiled. "Well, honey," he said, "I just thought you were trying, maybe, a little too hard. After all, Tessa, sometimes silence isn't such a terrifying thing."

Which brought Tessa immediately into silence. They drove to the Brown house on Pennsylvania Street just as the first few wet and enormous snowflakes began to descend. As they walked up the stone steps past two ridiculously imposing stone lions and then headed toward the rear of the property and the stables (where tour tickets and guidebooks were to be purchased), Tessa decided that she must be feverish, that clearly her wild-eyed run-on performance at lunch was only a symptom of impending illness and that the snow wasn't any great help, either. She was wearing flat shoes with very thin soles, and she knew instantly that the dampness gathering beneath her feet as she walked would be quickly transformed and transmitted and that by the end of the afternoon she'd undoubtedly be sniffling and perspiring and able to feel a rawness at the back of her throat.

Her father paid for their tour tickets and bought a souvenir guidebook (very small) and then, at Allie's insistence, bought replicas of old-time newspapers that contained the exploits, sayings, and deeds of the redoubtable Mrs. Brown. Together they left the coach house and slogged back through the increasing slush to the front of the house, where, they were told, they would be met by their guide.

This turned out to be a housewife. *Doing good work,* Tessa thought quickly and then apologized mentally to the woman. After all, why shouldn't someone devote her time to salvaging something she thought worthwhile? The woman—a petite, rather pretty lady in a long Victorian gown with ruffles and a high neck —explained that she was only one of many concerned citizens who were trying to recapture and restore some of Denver's exciting past. And that the Brown house was just the first and most important of history's footnotes that carried the notation "Denver, Colorado, U.S. of A." She invited the O'Connells to ask questions as they proceeded through the house, and said that anything she could do to make their visit more pleasant and informative was theirs for the asking.

From the very first moments of the tour, standing in the downstairs front hallway, Tessa was under stress. Some of it she identified as inner and self-generated; some of it came from the fact that standing there, listening politely as the woman from Historic Denver began to perform as she had been trained, it soon became clear that what the house held was less of Mrs. Brown and more of "the same period."

Which, to Tessa, meant she was listening to what might have been, or might soon be if the society was lucky in tracking it down. Which, to Tessa, wasn't good enough.

Their guide herself seemed to be somewhat embarrassed at being able to show them so little that was real, or that had been once actually owned and used by Mrs. Brown and her family. She apologized once, as they were standing in the doorway of the dining room. "So many pieces were sold or lost," she explained. "And the house itself has been used in so many incredibly different ways. Why once," she added, looking at Tessa and smiling in what Tessa took to be a conspirator's fashion, "the place was even used as a home for wayward young women."

Tessa nodded sympathetically and turned away, angry and insulted and patronized.

Mr. O'Connell asked polite questions as the quartet mounted a staircase to the second, and then the third, floors, and every so often something would catch Allie's eye and he, too, would ask as though he were really interested.

But the things, the pieces of furniture or the woodwork or the stained glass of which the woman was so proud, seemed to Tessa dull and uninteresting and lifeless. They didn't tell her anything about Mrs. Brown *or* about Denver in the "old days."

And she wasn't feeling well. Her stomach rolled and dipped and spun, and she had to unbutton her winter coat and take it off, carrying it from the second to the third floor. Her father had to remind her to put it on as they emerged later and started into the early winter darkness for their car.

Later, standing at the windows overlooking Cheesman Park, Tessa stared out at the city and decided that that Sunday was the last on which she would accompany both her father and Allie to some supposedly interesting, cultural, important event or spot. She had been alone, all day. Allie and her father joked and kidded and punched each other, just like guys from school, and Tessa realized suddenly that maybe boys just never grew out of being pals. But she, as a woman, how was she to react, to compete for attention

and affection? Lord knew, she had tried during lunch,
she thought. She had struggled to be bright and amusing and fun, even though admittedly she might have
overdone things. Then, when she had fallen silent during the afternoon, had anyone noticed? No. Allie and
her father must have just thought that silent was what
girls were best being. Quiet, unobtrusive, background.
Well, no more. If her father wanted to see her, he could
darn well see her—by herself.

She grinned into the reflection of herself at the window. One thing: she felt better. She had even announced
a totally ravenous hunger when they had returned
from the Brown house, ordering (as her father's eye-
brows raised and as he intoned his usual, "Better make
sure your eyes aren't bigger than your stomach, honey,") not only jumbo golden butterfly shrimp but *also*
egg rolls, and then, to top it all off, egg foo yong,
which was calculated to gum everything up in her in-
sides and linger for days and weeks and add at least
ten pounds.

She liked looking past herself, through herself, onto
the parkside below, even though the night lighting
made it difficult to see people or cars or buildings
precisely. The mountains in the west had become huge
black hulks on the horizon, dark enough to still be
differentiated against the almost equally black sky
above Denver, kept dusky by the city lights. In fact, she
liked being at No. 2 Cheesman Place. It made her feel
grand and important and rich and incredibly sophisticated, looking out at all of Denver that wasn't as fortunate as she.

She smiled into the glass, remembering that her
mother was somewhere below, on the ground looking
up instead of looking down.

The doorbell to the apartment sounded and Tessa
turned to watch her father hurry to the door, money in
hand, and then, after a brief exchange with a boy

who couldn't have been that much older than Tessa herself, return with his arms laden with Chinese food.

"Allie," Mr. O'Connell said loudly, "if you can tear yourself away from whatever it is you're watching, dinner's on."

Allie's disembodied voice was barely distinguishable over the television set in the small second bedroom. "Coming."

Tessa helped her father arrange the heavy paper containers around the dining room table and poured milk for herself and Allie. Mr. O'Connell refreshed his drink and returned to the table just as his son appeared. "Well, it ain't as good as my sainted mother made," said Mr. O'Connell with a laugh, "but I think it will do the job."

Tessa had already seated herself and was opening the packet in which her shrimp were. She daintily pulled two out by their tails. "Did they remember to add plum sauce?" she asked.

Mr. O'Connell explored the other containers and found a plastic sauce container. "Of course they did," he said. "They knew you dote on it."

Which was true. Tessa would have been perfectly happy putting plum sauce on Grape Nuts Flakes, if she'd been able.

The trio ate in comparative quiet: Tessa and Allie opening and examining and pulling things out of containers; Mr. O'Connell content to spoon out his chow mein onto a handful of crispy noodles and then, finished, to light a cigarette.

"I wonder what the Chinese do at Christmastime," he said finally. "I mean, if they have anything special like we do; you know, turkey and stuffing and cranberry sauce."

"I don't think they have Christmas, Dad," Allie said.

"Well, whatever their big holiday is, then," said Mr.

O'Connell. "Which reminds me," he went on, "Christmas and all. Anything special you two kids want?"

Tessa shook her head negatively and shrugged. She couldn't answer. Her mouth still held egg foo yong.

"Could I get a walkie-talkie set?" Allie asked. "Ferdy Watkins and I could really use one."

"He's a creep," Tessa managed.

"He's a genius," Allie defended hotly. "You're just jealous."

Tessa swallowed. "He's a freckle-faced little frog, and I agree with Mother. You see him entirely too often. He's not a good influence on you."

"I didn't call this meeting to listen to you two slice each other up," Mr. O'Connell interrupted with a smile.

"Well, Dad, could I have a walkie-talkie? Please?"

"You may consider that the matter is now under advisement."

Allie grinned wickedly at Tessa.

"You kids might be able to do something for me for Christmas, actually," said Mr. O'Connell.

"What?" asked Allie.

Tessa's stomach rumbled. "Pardon me," she said very quietly.

"It's not really a Christmas present or anything quite so simple," Mr. O'Connell began to explain. "It's just something happening, almost accidentally really, at this time of year, when we celebrate an old year's ending and a new one's beginning."

Tessa and Allie had nothing to say. They both waited.

"What I'd be very grateful to you both for," Mr. O'Connell said now quietly, almost hesitantly, "is if you could . . . well." He stopped and smiled embarrassingly. "This is harder than I thought," he said.

"Go on," Allie encouraged. "Tell us."

Mr. O'Connell nodded. "All right," he said. "I'm gong to get married again. And I want you both to be happy about it."

Allie's lower jaw fell and he stared at his father. Tessa put down her fork and sat straight up in her chair.

"I know you will be," Mr. O'Connell said quickly then, rushing on, tapping his cigarette against the side of an ashtray as he spoke and examining its ashes minutely. "I know you both want your mother and me to do what we feel is right and comfortable and best for us all. As for me, I've met someone I think is good for us all, someone you'll like, too."

"Are you asking our permission?" Allie wondered.

Mr. O'Connell laughed, tentatively. "In a way, I guess I am, Allie," he admitted.

Allie nodded and his face was somber. "I guess it's O.K.," he said. "If you're sure."

"I think you'll like her, Allie. She's pretty and bright and fun. And she has a wonderful laugh. And she's very adventuresome. She likes skiing and packing and horseback-riding. And she even knows something about walkie-talkies, I'll bet. If she doesn't, she will soon," Mr. O'Connell added.

"When are you going to do it?" Allie asked.

"Just before Christmas," said his father. He turned to face Tessa, who returned his look without expression, as though she were listening and understanding and yet had nothing to add or say or do, as though the news had no effect on her at all. "We want very much to give everyone a wonderful holiday, Tessa. We'd like to get married and spend a few days together, all of us, before the real holiday. Then we'll go off and take a little vacation ourselves. You and your mother will have Christmas together, just as I know you've planned. We don't want to run any kind of competition, you see."

Tessa nodded noncommittally.

"Actually, what this gives you both, in a way, is just

another family. Another happy place, I hope, where you can come and have fun and talk and share with us."

Tessa's gaze seemed to make her father uncomfortable. He looked away and stubbed out his cigarette.

"I want you both to understand something," Mr. O'Connell said in a low voice. "I'm still very, very fond of your mother. She's a wonderful woman. I'll always think that." He paused and sighed. "But, well, it's just what we talked about before. You know. Sometimes two people aren't in step any longer. They can both be talented and warm and considerate, but no matter how hard they try, somehow they've lost the sense of working together for things.

"There isn't going to be any competition, Tessa. You know that. My loyalties will always be with you and Allie, first." He coughed. "I mean, of course, as far as the two families go."

Tessa did not respond. She was pale. She pulled her hands down from the surface of the dining room table and held them tightly in her lap, her posture still ramrod straight and unforgiving.

"There's something else I wish you'd consider, kids," said Mr. O'Connell. "Of course, it's hard, I know. But what I'm saying, what I'm telling you about right now could just as well have come from your mother instead of me. I mean, well, it's only accidental that it's me who's found someone new to share my life with. She could have, first. Things just happened this way."

Tessa cleared her throat. "What is her name?" she asked at last, speaking clearly, one word at a time, carefully.

"Zandra."

Tessa sat motionless a moment and then nodded as though what her father said had only confirmed what she had known all along. She pushed her chair back from the table and stood, looking around a moment, seeing her coat thrown over the arm of a sofa in the living room.

She walked deliberately toward the couch and picked up her coat, her scarf, and her small leather purse.

"Tessa, don't," called her father, standing at the table and beginning to walk toward her. "If something troubles you, let's talk about it, please. We can work this all out. We can *all* be happy."

"Go right ahead," Tessa said, opening the apartment's front door. "You don't need me for that."

Allie muttered under his breath, "Dumb girl!"; her father said, "Damn!"; the front door slammed closed behind her.

7.

Have you ever had a week when all you can remember of it afterward is the sound of doors slamming?

Doors you slammed, to keep people out, or in. Doors other people slammed, to keep *you* in or out. Doors slamming just to mark with a tremendous sound-effect separation, or differences.

I will admit, my schoolwork took a sudden turn for the better. I became incredibly ambitious. My papers were on time; the tests and quizzes that reared their ugly heads were trifles, petty annoyances, and, to be truthful, petty triumphs; they really didn't mean anything. I even thought, although for only a minute or two, about asking the school librarian if I could be a sort of page during study hall. By the end of the week if a particular teacher asked a class a question and came up dry, automatically my name was called. Automatically I gave the right answer. How to lose friends and alienate people.

I didn't care. "Withdrawal" now means something to me.

Mostly what it means is coming across odd bits and pieces of information to which you say, on seeing them, "Hey, that's fantastic," and you rack your brains looking for a place in general daily life and conversation where you can drop what you've just read. You don't really retain this kind of fluff, not as far as I can tell. But I can't tell you how satisfying it is to sneak in something like, "Say, did you know that on the island of Maui you get only about three inches of rainfall annually on the eastern shore, but that in the mountains less than ten miles away you can sometimes have up to almost forty-seven feet of rain in the same year," into a totally offhand consideration of a Denver day.

Or just try to casually include the fact that the Homestead Act was passed by Congress in 1862 promising a hundred sixty acres of land to any head of a family after he had cleared and improved the land and had lived on it for five years when one of your friends announces she is about to move into a new house or something.

I'm not at all certain that this kind of sudden inspiration means anything to anyone else, but it all has the peculiar effect of making you feel at one and the same time astonishingly well-informed and amazingly stupid.

Still, picking up odds and ends of history or biography or just random data sort of punctuates the kind of week I'm talking about, where the periods in your life are all made of the sound of a door slamming.

Something else that kept running through my mind just then. Since it was nearly Christmas and all, I mean. Whatever happened to the promises that if you were a good little girl, especially as the holiday approached, your every wish would come true on Christmas morning? Santa Claus was bound to reward someone who had eaten all her vegetables, had cleaned her room without being asked (mine was spotless that week, believe me), did her homework and brought home good grades, helped around the house without being commanded, was obedient and quiet and considerate?

I'm not at all sure what this means, but the answer to the above in my mind was, "The way of all flesh."

I wasn't entirely alone in my blue funk. I made two trips downtown to see Our Lady of the Sorrows. The first time there I got in a good ten or twelve minutes of very intense empathy, and had almost begun to feel better, to feel myself sort of rising a little above everything that surrounded me on the outside, before a group of very well-dressed and *very* hard-heeled matrons from some southeast suburb came bustling through with a museum guide to *ooh* and *ahh* and in general behave as though they were a gaggle of geese on the loose for the first and only time.

The second time was a little more successful. It was the only time in my whole career I ever skipped school. What I did was I just stayed on the bus, and when it turned westward on Colfax I simply sat where I was. It was a sudden decision, I guess, but I must have been thinking about it all morning because I didn't feel any panic at all.

I got to the museum a little early, actually before it opened. I huddled near the wind tunnel awhile and soon enough we (there were maybe a dozen other people there, too, probably college kids or something) were let in. I went straight up to the third floor.

But when I got into the little chapel, getting into the right mood wasn't quite as easy as I'd expected. I had to almost ignore my little doll-like friend. Maybe it was because, for some reason, I was mad, angry I should say, and that doesn't exactly lead easily into being spiritual. So I studied some of the other glass cases in the little room and began to wonder just what exactly the Penitentes did in their services. There were hints in some of the notations alongside the art objects that sort of gave you the shivers. I mean, apparently part of their devotions included self-flagellation. Which simply means beating yourself.

I remembered seeing a movie once, way back when television was still mostly black-and-white. It was a Swedish movie, subtitled (which on a television set is impossible anyway), and what I remember best about it was a scene of a religious procession in the countryside, along a dusty, rocky road. The believers were on their knees, some of them, getting bloodied and scarred and you had to think that they didn't really feel anything, so intense were their feelings for the pilgrimage. There were witches in the procession, too, in carts (tumbrels, those are called), bound and wounded and clearly set up for a burning. And behind, to the rear of the hundreds of penitents and believers, were people whipping themselves. Some did it sort of gingerly, even though these in particular still wore cloaks or coats and the little, thin birch sticks they used couldn't really have hurt them all that much. Others, though, were really cutting themselves. Some had whips of leather, with little round-looking balls attached or studs. These people were the grubbiest. Mud-streaked, tear-streaked, bloodstained, and the welts and lacerations on their backs were terrible to see.

And yet they too gave you the feeling that they couldn't actually *feel* the pain. That what they were doing was lost in a kind of divine ecstasy, a sort of spirit-lifting madness that left their bodies below on the rocks and sand while their hearts and minds soared somewhere above, pushed ever higher by each blow they struck themselves.

Maybe this was why, when I went finally to stand before the case that held my friend, there were tears in her eyes. I mean, maybe she was watching one of those medieval processions right here in our own country just a hundred or so years ago (actually a little more than that, I know), and her heart was breaking for the people who crawled and felt their way along their own kind of road to Calvary. Maybe she understood what her fellow Penitentes wanted, to scourge themselves because of guilt for letting Christ die on the cross.

And maybe, above all else, she knew too that all those people in pain and sorrow weren't to blame after all. (I've never believed in the idea of original sin, which says you're sinful from the moment you're born because of what Adam did in the garden of Eden, and you can't escape it. After all, the most harmless, most innocent thing in the whole world is a baby, isn't it?)

Anyway, her eyes were full. That morning, in my own mind, I guess, they were fuller than ever before because she knew *we* were not to blame. That troubles and pain and sorrow are a part of everyone's life, and that you can't ever hope to ease them by blaming yourself. No matter how devout you are, how often you go to church, how strongly you believe in *anything,* you can walk right out of church and be hit by a car. It isn't all judgment or anything like that. It's just life.

And then it really did hit me that maybe that was why she was tearful. That maybe just because Life was like that—unforgiving, surprising, unexpected, sometimes grand and happy and sometimes mean and low —that people were to be pitied and prayed for because they insisted on trying to figure it all out. And it can't be figured.

I don't exactly know what a "religious experience" is, but I think I got as close to that as I'm ever going to get that morning. I can't tell you too much about it, except that it came to a rather sudden and embarrassing stop. I remember three things, probably not all happening at the same precise moment, but then again maybe they did.

I was standing before her case, looking up into her face, and I too must have been crying. I remember hearing myself say something like "Oh, you're right, it *is* sad. But it's only human, isn't it? And *that's* what makes it so sad, isn't it? That's why you're crying," and I remember seeing my own hand reach up toward her face and sort of try to stroke her cheek, or even maybe just pat her hair softly, gently. And then I remember someone's hand on *my* head, and on my shoulder. Someone very gentle with a soft, but masculine, voice, saying slowly, over and over again, "Please, miss. It's not allowed."

I remember turning suddenly, red in the face, knowing after a second where I was and who, and seeing a guard from the museum standing right there, his hand still on my shoulder, patting it with real concern. He wasn't handsome or anything (he was about sixty, I'd guess), but he too seemed sort of stunned by what was going on. He had his job to do and he knew he had to be firm, but he was so—so loving about it.

I pulled my hand down from the glass and started to say, "I'm sorry," but before I could even get *that* out, he was shaking his head and his shiny black face told me not to apologize. All he said was, "That's better. Thank you. Be more careful, miss, will you?"

I nodded and I didn't feel at all embarrassed anymore. And without another word, or even another look back to make sure that I wasn't going to attack the frame the minute he left the chapel, he walked out into another gallery.

I buttoned my coat and hurried out of the museum and went back to dear old East High. And all the way back on the bus all I could think was how lucky I had been to find someone so kind, so *human* just then when something inside me needed just exactly that.

I wasn't quite myself that afternoon in class. "Ethereal" (meaning otherworldly, light, celestial) was the only word I can think of that probably comes closest to describing the way I was behaving. (Also, if you had been there to label me yourself, probably "dumb"!) Charlotte, always the observer, caught me between Chemistry and English and in a whisper of considerable urgency demanded an immediate audience at the end of the day. I nodded, I suppose. It really didn't matter any to me, and I suppose in my state of highly refined sensibility, I assumed that *she* was in some sort of trouble and needed to confide in *me*.

Which is why her assault really took me by surprise.

"What on earth is the matter with you?" said she, not wasting a moment on preliminaries.

"Nothing," I said. "What's the matter with you?"

"You are."

"Meaning?"

"Just that I've watched you float through the halls all afternoon and positively dream your way through class. Are you practicing for sainthood or what?"

I smiled condescendingly. And I kept walking, through the hallway out toward the bus stop.

"If you must know, Charlotte, just at this very time I have a lot on my mind. Rather distressing, some of it." I sighed and looked (but only for a second!) skyward. Dramatically I huddled my books and purse then and kept walking, head down, a serene expression on my face that couldn't begin to be interpreted.

Charlotte just kept pace and didn't say a word. Which infuriated me. "I'm not quite sure you could understand," I said. "Or help."

Still she refused to bite. Well, I wasn't going to lure

her any further. If she really was my friend, sooner or later she'd just have to ask me questions.

Which she did as we settled into our seats on the bus.

"All right, Tessa," she began. "I'm all primed now. Go ahead. Just what is so distressing?"

It wasn't the kind of sympathetic inquiry I'd imagined, but I decided to take it anyway. Actually, I really think I did need to talk about it all just then.

"My father is getting married again." That was it, plain and ungarnished.

"When did you find out?" Charlotte asked, turning rather quickly in her seat and grabbing my hands.

"Last Sunday. But I knew, Charlotte. I knew before."

"Who's the woman? Is it someone we know?"

I lied. "No."

Charlotte sighed and squeezed my hands understandingly. "Are you *very* hurt?" she asked softly. "I mean, do you feel rejected and abandoned?"

I looked up at her. "Not at all," I said quickly. "After all, Charlotte, this isn't all that difficult to handle. I mean, we're all old enough to understand these things. He needs someone and he found someone. It has nothing to do with Allie and me. Nothing *against* us, I mean. Surely you can understand that."

"Well, if you *can* adjust to it, whatever's making you so peculiar?"

"For one thing, Charlotte, it *does* mean readjusting. I mean, suddenly I'm supposed to have two families and each is supposed to be treated equally and I'm supposed to love everyone. I mean, it's not easy being forced to look at someone you hardly know and imagine them as a parent."

"You're not supposed to look at them equally," Charlotte said. "Surely, his new wife will come only *after* your mother. I mean, you can't just desert her."

"Like my father, you mean?"

"Ah hah!" Charlotte crowed. "That's it! You're concerned about your mother's feelings of rejection."

"Don't sound like a pint-sized Freud, please."

"But I'm right, aren't I?"

"Well," I said, thinking it out a little. "In a way. Even though we all agree that two people who can't get on any longer should live apart, still and all it's awfully soon to have found someone else. I mean it's almost an insult to my mother. He lived with her for years and years and had us and everything was supposed to have been fine and dandy all that time, and suddenly in he walks and, in effect, just announces that it's taken him almost no time at all to find someone else, someone new, or better, or just as important. It can't be very easy, taking that news, I mean."

We had to get up and transfer then. Which meant that Charlotte, with her common-sense approach to life, had to keep her own counsel for a few minutes. (Let me tell you, fond though I am, that nothing is more aggravating than listening to someone run on about common sense and reality and decision-making, especially when that someone is taller than you are. And, worse, many times right.)

We got settled on the Colorado Avenue bus and headed northward.

"Have you talked with your mom about it?" Charlotte asked as soon as she was comfortable.

"No. Not yet. I'm not sure she's ready to."

"Do you think it would help if together we talked to her about it? I mean, it might just take out some of the sting."

"Absolutely not!"

"Well, Tessa, you can't just ignore it. And you can't protect her, either, can you?"

"Yes, I can," I answered. Actually, I hadn't thought about protecting my mother before, but the idea seemed now natural and well-intentioned. "I can make the whole thing easier for her, if I really try. I mean, give her lots of reassurance, you know. Let her know she's still number one in my mind."

"Will that satisfy her?"

"That's a mean question!"

"Still, it won't, will it? If she's feeling abandoned and lost, you're not the heaviest anchor, or the best escape hatch, or whatever."

"Well, I will be!" I defended. "I can be as soft and gentle and considerate as anyone else. I mean, just think, she gave that man the best years of her life and now she's been thrown out with the rest of the junk he'd collected in his life. It just isn't fair."

Charlotte sat silently a moment. Then, very quietly, she spoke. "Tessa, *you* don't feel that you're the junk that's been discarded, do you?"

"I've already told you, of course not! Besides, Daddy's already promised us that he still puts us, Allie and me, in first place and always will. I'm thinking about Mother."

Charlotte nodded, as though unconvinced. "One thing," she said. "Maybe his new wife will be nice. I mean, that would make things easier, wouldn't it? Sooner or later, since Denver isn't the biggest town in the whole world, they'll all meet. Maybe they'll even like each other, your mother and his new wife. Maybe your mother can even see her and sort of understand the—the attraction. I mean, that's a very sensible approach, isn't it? Understanding the differences between yourself and someone else, and sort of learning to value them."

"His new 'wife,'" I said without really thinking, "is a whore!"

"Tessa!"

I sat a moment, hating myself. Not for thinking what I thought, but for letting it out.

Charlotte gripped my arm suddenly. "You *do* know, don't you?" she said breathlessly. "That's why you're so upset."

"I don't know what you're talking about."

"Tessa O'Connell, you do, too! You know who the woman is and you hate her!"

"No such thing."

"Were they having an affair? All that time? Oh, Tessa, I'm so sorry I didn't understand before. Gee, this must be just hell for you!"

"Charlotte, you don't know what you're talking about. And neither do I. I know almost nothing about her. And I don't want to know. But I'll tell you one thing, if my father thinks he can just come round Sunday after Sunday and somehow behave as though he's a full-time father, he's very much mistaken. If he thinks I have to feel the same way about him now as I used to, especially after he's married, he's in for a big surprise!"

Charlotte sat motionless as I gathered myself and my stuff together. (I got off the bus before she did.) I stood and tried to get by her, but she wouldn't turn her knees.

"Tessa, now listen. It seems to me that if everything you say is true, you're the only adult on the scene. You've just got to take control, that's all. I mean, I think shielding your mom is absolutely the right thing to do." She paused. "Just one thing, though."

"I'll miss my stop!"

"I don't care. I just want to say that, for everyone's sake, if somehow—even though I *know* this probably wouldn't happen—if somehow you're wrong about . . . about everything, don't fight it."

"What on earth does *that* mean?"

"Suppose your father's new wife is really a good woman," Charlotte said. "Don't hold it against her."

"You make about as much sense as Allie when he talks in his sleep!"

Walking home, I suddenly felt incredibly capable. My mother needed me. It was a nice feeling. Even nicer than that was the feeling I had that I could give her what she did need: love and care and feeling and understanding. And safety.

8.

"Tessa, you simply have to get up now. Your father will be here in less than an hour."

Tessa lay curled on her side, her face to the window, the covers still bunched up around her shoulders. "I think I'm coming down with something," she said, muffling her voice against her pillow.

"Like what?" asked her mother, walking to the side of the bed and looking down at her. "Have you a fever?"

"No," Tessa said weakly. "But I think I'm going to."

"That's ridiculous!" said her mother with a little laugh. "Come on now, up you get! Allie's already showered so the bathroom's yours."

Mrs. O'Connell leaned down and quickly, with no warning, pulled the sheets and blankets away from Tessa's body. "What you *will* get is pneumonia unless you get cracking and get dressed."

Tessa forced herself to sit up, cross-legged. "Mother, do you think it would be O.K. if sometimes, not all the time but just every so often, I called you 'Dorie'? I mean, would you mind?"

Mrs. O'Connell turned at the door to the bedroom

and smiled. "I wouldn't mind, Tessa, but what brings this on?"

"Nothing," Tessa said softly. "I just thought, you know, when we sometimes . . . have talks and all, it just might be more . . . more natural, you know? I mean, two women sitting together and everything, talking."

Mrs. O'Connell's face was composed. She wore solid-gray wool slacks and a multicolored, printed ski sweater. Tessa waited for her answer, thinking to herself how pretty her mother *still* was, and briefly she felt grateful that she resembled her mother as much as she did.

"Honey, I don't mind at all, if you feel it's important. But I am rather curious about those 'talks' you mention. Have I missed anything? Are we going to have one now? This very morning?"

Tessa leaned back against her bedstead and the pillows there. "Well," she said seriously, "a lot of things are happening right now, aren't they? Apart from Christmas, I mean."

Mrs. O'Connell folded her arms beneath her breasts. "You mean with Daddy?" she asked.

Tessa nodded. "But it's not just him. I mean, what he's doing changes us all, doesn't it?"

"Not really, dear," said Tessa's mother, moving to Tessa's bed and sitting at the foot of it.

"How can you say that?" Tessa asked. "Of course it does. For one thing, I mean the very least, suddenly there's another woman around."

Mrs. O'Connell looked into her daughter's eyes without blinking. "These things happen, Tessa. You know that."

Tessa nodded. "Of course I do," she said, "but it's only now beginning to hit me what it all means. To you."

"Which would be what?" her mother asked.

Tessa stared down at her crossed ankles. She couldn't understand why she suddenly felt embarrassed, as though no matter what she said, her mother would merely accept, not discuss or argue or explain away. "Well, I mean," Tessa said haltingly, "the hurt and all."

Mrs. O'Connell sat silently a moment. Then she nodded, as if to herself. "Tessa, part of being hurt is allowing yourself to be hurt," she said. "Of course what Daddy's doing bothers me. I'd be fibbing if I said it didn't. But I'm not going to be hurt by it, or damaged. Any further than I have already been."

"But that's just exactly what I mean!" Tessa exclaimed. Then she lowered her voice. "I *know* how much strength it must take," she said, and then added experimentally, "Dorie. How much determination to stay cool."

Mrs. O'Connell smiled at her daughter. "You're a sweet girl, Tessa."

"Well, I just wanted you to know that if, well, if sometimes you sort of had to unload, let some of it out or anything, I mean, well, you can count on me."

Mrs. O'Connell nodded and grinned. "I think you ought to know, Tessa, that even to myself I don't picture myself a wronged woman."

Tessa was astonished. "You don't? I don't see how you could avoid that."

"Well, be that as it may, dear, I don't. After all, if life had been led a little differently, who knows? Perhaps I might have been the one to announce another marriage."

"Mother, you couldn't!"

"Why not, Tessa? Whatever needs I had when I married your father I still have. I'm a little older, of course, and hopefully a little smarter. But what seemed worthwhile to me way back when still seems worthwhile today. Working together, caring about the same things, bringing a family up." Mrs. O'Connell paused and reached out for one of Tessa's hands. "What would you have thought if I had come home one day and said you were going to have a new stepfather."

Tessa thought. " 'New' stepfather means I would have already have had one," she avoided.

"You know what I mean," Mrs. O'Connell said. "What would you have thought?"

"I don't know."

"Wouldn't you have felt happy for me, Tessa?"

"I guess. Probably depends on who it was."

"But that's unfair, dear. If I meet someone I love, someone I'm proud of and someone I want *you* to love, wouldn't you at least give him a chance?"

"But what if I didn't like him?" Tessa asked. "Would that make a difference to you? Would you give him up?"

Mrs. O'Connell answered without taking a second's pause. "No."

"You wouldn't? But that's incredibly selfish!"

"No, it isn't. Not if *I* felt he was worth a world to me. Tessa, since you seem to be ready to look at things and discuss them like this, then you're old enough to understand that sometimes, not often but still it can happen, sometimes a woman with children, or even a man, simply has to grab what she loves regardless. Of course, if I ever did remarry, I'd want you and Allie to be happy for me, *and* to like your stepfather, at least. Admire him, perhaps. Find him interesting and fun. Be able in time to confide in him, to think of him as one of your best friends. But even if you never could, and the man still pleased me, I'm rather afraid, dear, my loyalties and dreams and affection would still be his first."

"But what about us?"

"I'd love you, too, Tessa. Just as before. But, after all, dear, you're getting to an age where your real life is about to begin. Just as you wouldn't want me to lay down a load of rules and regulations that wouldn't any longer fit, or would have to do with parts of your life that are none of my business, I can't have you doing the same, or trying to, to me. Now can I?"

"I guess not."

Mrs. O'Connell patted her daughter's hand. "I still love your father, Tessa. But differently now. He's part of my life, and he always will be. But when we separated he became a part of my past life, not my future one. Oh, I know, sometimes I get angry, and sometimes I sound as though I'm hurt. Sometimes, even, I might cry a little, feeling sorry for myself or for you kids. But you have to expect that. I mean, that's what one has at the end of a relationship like this, sadness and regret. Happily, I also have you and Allie. I don't need to tell you how important either of you are to me, do I?"

Tessa didn't reply. Somehow the kind of talk she'd imagined having with her mother had changed its character. Instead of being between two equals, two women who understood each other and supported each other, here *again* was a mother talking *to* a daughter. It was very disappointing.

Worse, it hadn't offered an escape.

"Oh, wow!" Allie whispered, looking out the front-seat window as his father stopped the car in the driveway. "Is this where you're going to live?"

The house on Race Street was dusky, dark brick, set well back from the curb and further camouflaged by a stand of firs that marched across the lawn single file. The sunlight that bounced off the isolated patches of snow on the grass reflected against this evergreen wall, making the house itself seem even darker and more imposing by contrast.

"It looks grander than it really is, Allie," said Mr. O'Connell.

"Wow!"

Allie opened his car door and stood a moment, staring, before he closed it. Tessa took a big breath and pushed down the handle of her own door and got out.

"It's quite close to Cheesman Place, isn't it?" she said quietly.

"Yes, as a matter of fact it's been very handy," admitted her father with a broad smile.

Tessa held in her own response. Determinedly.

"Well, let's do it, kids," Mr. O'Connell said. "Lunch'll be cold if we don't start soon."

He waited for Tessa to come around the front end of car and then, as though determined to form a family grouping that might have been perfect for an advertisement of some kind, Mr. O'Connell put an arm around Allie's shoulder and an arm around Tessa's, and together they crossed the lawn to a flagstone path leading to the house's front door.

Without ringing or waiting to knock, Mr. O'Connell pushed open the heavy oak door and shouted into the house, "Zandra! Your subjects await without!"

"Without what?" was the reply in a light, laughing female voice that preceded its owner into the hallway. "I can supply whatever it is you need as long as I know what it *is!*"

She was thin, fashionably so, Tessa saw, and dressed with a kind of careful carelessness that, on another woman, Tessa would have envied. Her hair was longish and lightly frosted, its real light brown blending more toward a gold because of it. Her complexion was astonishingly clear, and her features were nearly evenly perfect. Objectively, Tessa admitted that this was an attractive woman, even more up close. That time before, when she had seen her father talking with her at the club, Tessa had only been able to guess at the overall woman: slim, talkative, laughing, touching. But it had been so clear, so obvious to everyone, and yet Tessa's mother hadn't even begun to understand.

A hand was thrust out at Tessa. "Hi, Tessa," she said. "I'm Zandra Stenner. I'm glad you could come to lunch. And I'm crazy about your dad."

Tessa nodded noncommittally. "Hello," she said, pulling her hand quickly back from the older woman's.

"Allie?" Zandra asked. Instead of shaking hands with him, she impulsively (*maybe,* Tessa thought) put an arm around his shoulder and hugged him into her body. "Gosh, I'm glad I'm getting two men instead of just one."

Allie blushed.

Zandra pulled away from the boy and melted into Mr. O'Connell's shoulder. "He's adorable," she laughed. "And he's modest, not at all like some people I know!"

"Come on, kids, shuck your coats," said Mr. O'Connell with a grin. "I *assume* we're staying for lunch."

Tessa took hers off and handed it to her father, who hung it in a dark hall closet as Allie struggled out of his and walked behind his father and handed it to him. "There!" said Mr. O'Connell. "I think we're set now. Where's the band?"

"No band, but we can at least have a drink in the library," said Zandra. "A little wine for the kids, if they'd like."

Allie hovered near his father as the quartet left the hallway and walked through a sizable formal living room into a smaller, cozier bookcase-lined room whose colors were bright and yet soothing at the same time. Tessa stayed a pace behind the others, trying as she walked to gauge and estimate and examine everything. She stood at the entrance to the small den, watching her father and Zandra help each other at the bar there, and thought angrily to herself, *Who says crime doesn't pay?*

"Tessa?" Zandra was holding a wine goblet out to her, full of a white wine. "Would you like a cube of ice in yours?"

Tessa nodded, without smiling. If Zandra Stenner was

porcelain, her own mother, Dorie, was earthenware. It wasn't fair.

"You sure have a lot of books," Allie said, looking momentarily uncomfortable and uncertain whether to stand or sit.

"Do you like to read, Allie?" Zandra asked politely, making the decision for him by taking his hand and making him sit beside her on a leather couch.

"Some stuff," Allie muttered, eyes down.

"Like what?" Mrs. Stenner asked.

"Space stuff," Allie answered. "Science, you know. And . . . and biography, too, once in a while."

"We have hundreds of biographies here," Zandra exclaimed happily. "Everyone from that crazy emperor Nero who loved to play with matches to John F. Kennedy. You'll have a field day here, I'll bet."

Mr. O'Connell carried his drink to where Tessa was standing and stopped beside her, putting his arm again over her shoulder and looking back with a smile at Zandra and Allie on the couch. "Tessa's the scholar, though," he said. "Allie reads to learn how and why, but Tessa wants to uncover the when and what next. I've been graced by two very intelligent offspring."

Zandra turned sympathetically toward Tessa and her father. There was an impish gleam in her eyes. "No doubt the influence of their mother, actually," she said and laughed teasingly.

"I would never deny it," Mr. O'Connell replied.

"Tessa, won't you come over here and sit down with us?" Zandra wondered, patting the cushion on her left.

Tessa's father lifted his arm from her shoulders. Tessa had no choice.

"There, that's better," Zandra said as Tessa settled herself. "Now, for just one very tiny minute, if you'll permit me, I want to be serious. Not drear and boring!" She laughed suddenly and then as suddenly stopped. "But serious."

Tessa looked at her hands in her lap, one holding her glass, still not tasted.

"I want both of you to know," Zandra said quietly, "that I *am* in love with your father. That I think I can make him very, very happy. And that I never, ever want you to feel there is any kind of competition between me and your mother. I know how wonderful a woman she is, and what a really fine job she's done bringing you both along. I admire her and I want you to know that."

Tessa raised her eyes and looked across the small room at her father's face: shining, clear-eyed, proud. She'd never before imagined him as a sex object, or tried to diagnose the appeal he might once have held for her mother.

Apparently Allie then felt it was necessary to make some sort of family reply. "O.K.," he said.

"Thank you, Allie," Zandra said evenly. Tessa felt as though something in that short sentence had been aimed at her, but she had no intention of acknowledging it.

"Really," Zandra continued, "I don't even want to be considered your stepmother. That's a horrid title, and every time I hear of it I keep thinking of Snow White!"

That fits, Tessa thought.

"Ideally, I'd just like to be the woman your father married, someone I *hope* you'll think is nice and fun and not *too* embarrassing. I'll try to be considerate and helpful. If I learn to love you a little, too, as we go along, I hope you won't hold that against me."

"O.K.," Allie inserted a second time.

Zandra turned to look at Tessa. Tessa held her eyes steady and pretended to smile. But she knew it looked forced.

"*Now,*" Mr. O'Connell said with an enormous, dramatic sigh, "do you think you could feed us starving vagabonds?"

Zandra laughed and stood up from the couch. "

can't think what's keeping Bunch," she said, walking to the doorway of the library and calling loudly, "Bunch! Lunch!" She turned with a silly grin. "I never heard that quite that way before," she blushed.

Mr. O'Connell laughed and went to Zandra's side and gave her a quick kiss on the tip of her nose.

"Who's Bunch?" Allie asked.

Zandra peered around Mr. O'Connell's shoulder. "I'll bet your father told you Bunch's real name, instead, didn't he?"

"What's that?" Allie wanted to know.

"Frances," came a disembodied reply in a girl's voice with half a groan attached.

Tessa looked up as Bunch Stenner slipped out from behind where her own mother and Mr. O'Connell stood in the doorway.

"Hi, Tessa," Fran Stenner said, aiming her greeting across the room almost timidly.

Tessa's eyes widened for just a fraction of a second and her stomach felt suddenly hollow. The girl she looked at was the girl she knew, slightly, as part of the Jennie Munson-Fran Stenner-"O.K." McCall trio, and for which she had neither love nor admiration.

"Hi, Fran," she said finally. She *had* to say something.

9.

What I really need is a hobby. Something I can turn to when I want to lose myself, when I don't any longer want to keep thinking the same thoughts, or about the same things.

Winter, of course, forbids gardening. Which is really too bad in a way, because gardening means you have to learn about seeds and plants and how they grow, but even better it offers one activity that is practically mindless: weeding. Which you can do for hours and is absolutely endless (unlike cleaning windows, for example, because when *that's* done, that's done).

I could try to persuade myself that there is a career waiting for me in medicine, or maybe in nuclear physics. But I can't stand scientific things. Worse, I can't even understand them. I mean, it seems to me plain and simple that the weight of an airplane, to take one example, should be so great that it could never even *think* of getting off the ground. What I mean is, the *end* of an airplane. What keeps it from just dragging along the ground as it tries to take off, is what I don't understand.

Besides, careers like medicine or nuclear anything are sort of selfless. Which I'm not. And also, which is even more off-putting, everyone who works in something like this plays chess. To relax! I can't even beat Allie. My problem is that while I know where all the men go, I can't ever see them except as individuals. I don't have the ability to see what my father would call "the big picture."

And unless something really grabs you, staying ahead in school is like cleaning windows. So that's out.

Which all adds up to being positively *condemned* to replay all those scenes that drive you crazy.

Which I did a lot, right after that first time at Zandra's.

I also did other things. For example, I stopped speaking to my younger brother—may he be stolen by gypsies!

The reason for that was that he was so incredibly stupid and gullible. Imagine, being taken in by all that smiling and laughing and teasing and the positively disgusting show of real, genuine interest in him. In him! As though he were some extraordinary sort of unique genius, where everything he said was worth thinking about, hard, or asking to learn more!

Actually, though, I supposed Allie just wasn't old enough, or worldly-wise, to understand how he was being used.

Of course *I* was old enough, and did understand.

Not that I didn't dissemble. I smiled, after a while. And I spoke when spoken to. And I even complimented her on the lunch, although under duress. (Which is to say, my father forced it from me. "Isn't this something, Tessa?" Well, virtually, there was no way out.) I even allowed Fran to take me around the house on a sort of tour, and said some dumb appropriate thing about her room when I saw that, too.

One good thing: she was as distressed by all this as I was. I could tell. I mean, while her mother was coming on like gangbusters, smiling and laughing and being interested and helpful, Fran just sat there almost exactly as I did, nodding just a little or forcing a more pleasant expression onto her face. I couldn't tell if she thought Daddy wasn't good enough for her mother, or if she was afraid of losing some of her mother's attention with more of us around, even though it might be sort of rare and all. I mean, we didn't *plan* to pretend to be a "family."

And I for one certainly didn't plan to be around all that much, either. The way I saw it, if this thing absolutely was going to happen regardless of the way any of us felt, then my father, already just a "Sunday father," would become a sort of distant relative. The kind you always have to force yourself to sit down and write thank-you notes to after a holiday. Someone you see maybe a couple of times a year. I had no intention of deserting my mother in her hour of need. Furthermore, I didn't need anything from them—most especially not from her! It was all I could do to even pick at the food she gave us. (Whatever happened to the ancient and very wise custom of having a food-taster accompany you around? Like when someone's a king or queen or something, with spies and assassins all over, and people just breathless to knock you off and then take over your place, whatever it is. Actually, I didn't think she'd try to poison Allie or me. At least, not right away. Maybe when she got to know us better?)

Of course, it was disruptive. For us all. I mean, we would all have to start suddenly including in our plans for everyday living a whole bunch of new things, new people. And we all have to decide, although in Allie's case I'm sure it would be unconsciously, just how far to go with each other, how much to share, to open up with, to talk about.

It's peculiar. I'm certain Fran didn't intend to start taking me under her wing, for example. In school or out. After all, in her own mind, she was older and more sophisticated, and her attitudes about some things totally different than mine. (I think I mentioned this earlier.)

There's also the little matter of competition. Which really didn't exist. Yet.

Naturally we were different. But in more than just ideas. Even in looks. I mean, I'm more your everyday all-American type. You know: bright, alert, pretty, open. Fran, on the other hand, has a sort of *foreignness* about her. I can't explain this too well right now. Just that she's terrifically slim but not skinny, has dark hair that's long enough to be fashionable but not too long to get tangled and frizzy. She has dark, dark eyes that seem very distant sometimes, as though she's actually only visiting the planet temporarily and her mind's frequently being called back to some distant and weird civilization.

I'm not sure she's fantastically smart. In school, I

guess, she gets along. But it seems to me that some-one who tries so hard to be "alluring" to the other sex can't be all that secure or all that intelligent. After all, with the world opening up the way it is today, a woman can do and be a lot more than just some man's playmate. If she *thinks* she can.

At that moment, everything was sort of in limbo. Be-tween Fran and me. Between Daddy and us. Between us ourselves.

For example, Allie turned out to be incredibly insen-sitive just about then. Take when Daddy brought us home last Sunday. Naturally, to be even minimally po-lite, Mother had to ask us about the day. How we liked Zandra, the house, Fran.

If you consider for a minute that Allie's only eleven, I guess his enthusiasm was at least partially understand-able.

"She's got a huge house!" he starts right off, ignoring completely the fact that what we have is the positive best that Mother could do for us, now anyway. "It's got about six bedrooms," he barrels ahead, "and one of them is going to be mine when I stay there, and she's promised I can decorate it the way I want. I can even take a part of the attic, if I want, and make a sort of clubhouse out of it, which is super!"

Being the klutz he is, he hurries right on, ignoring the perfectly plain fact that everything he says is an ar-row in my mother's heart.

"And there's enough room in the back yard for a swimming pool, and Daddy says that as soon as I get my junior life saving we'll think about putting one in. Wouldn't that be great?

"And the yard's got all kinds of super-fantastic hiding places, and dugouts, and Ferdy and I have already de-cided to—"

I couldn't stand it any longer. "Ferdy!" I interrupted.

"Yes, Ferdy," Allie defended. "He's my very best friend."

"That's like having a shark as a pet!"

"You're just jealous!" Allie pronounces like an idiot. "There isn't one person you know who's as smart as he is."

"Happily."

"Hey, come on, you two. Tessa, unless you want Allie to be critical of all your friends, it isn't really fair to be unkind to his."

"Yeah," said Allie. Which is about the sum of his intellect.

"Actually," I said, lowering my voice and deciding to ignore the redheaded cross Life handed me, "the house isn't all that grand."

My mother leaned back in the corner of the sofa and waited.

"I mean, sure, it's a little bigger and all, but also it's terribly dark and heavy-feeling. You know what I mean? And there really isn't the same feeling of . . . of comfort there we have here, Mom. Not at all. I mean, there are some chairs you'd be positively terrified of sitting on for fear they'd crack right under you. And the place is absolutely jammed with antiques, all kinds of junk. Which, I suspect, is what a lot of it is."

"Oh?" said Mother, a little smile breaking on her face.

"Worse, I think she has abysmal taste. Not at all as good or as sensible as yours, Mom. Basically, even, just think how silly it is to even live like she does. I mean, for two people who needs all that room? It must be incredibly expensive to keep up and all. Probably it takes all the money she has just to keep going." I took a breath. "Really, she could learn a lot from you, if you want to know what I think."

"Do you?" asked my mother quietly, with a little nod.

"And she's not nearly as attractive as you are," I said. "Not really. Oh, there's a certain way she has, you know, but it's mostly good makeup, and long skirts. Actually, she's sort of horsy-looking, if you want to know."

"No, she isn't!" Allie said.

"Shut up," I told him. "She certainly is. And probably terribly spoiled as well. I mean, I'm sure she'd never have the sense of pulling together or helping that you do, Mother. Never."

My mother smiled again. "How was lunch?"

"Super!" Allie exclaimed.

"If you're fond of premixed sauces," I added.

My mother laughed and folded her leg under her. "And what about Fran, then?" she asked.

"Bunch is super!" Allie said instantly. What else.

"Bunch?" asked my mother.

"That's her nickname," Allie explained. "She hates being called Frances."

"I think it's a pretty name," Mother said.

"Well, she doesn't," Allie supplied.

"Tessa?"

"What?"

"How do you feel about Fran? You knew her before, didn't you?"

"Vaguely."

"Well, now that—that you two are going to be a little closer, did you like her?"

"What happened to her father?" Allie interrupted.

"I don't know, dear," Mother answered.

"I wonder if he was killed or anything," Allie said. "In Vietnam."

"You know as much as I do," said my mother. "But it's not easy, you know, bringing up a child alone."

"Maybe they were divorced," I said.

"Oh!" Allie said. "You mean Bunch is a product of a broken home? Wow!"

"That's not such an unusual thing, Allie," my mother said. "If it's true."

"And aren't we all?" I added sarcastically. "Thank goodness we're able to take care of ourselves."

My mother turned to look at me and didn't speak for a moment. I couldn't actually tell what she was thinking.

I need hardly add that for the next few days, whenever he thought of it, Allie put a knife in my mother's back. How terrific everything at *her* house was; how glad Bunch was to have a brother; how Zandra had promised to take us all skiing at Vail; how even Ferdy thought Daddy was getting something pretty hot. This last we needed like a hole in the head!

I spent most of my time trying to outguess and head Allie off every time he opened his mouth. Once I even tried to explain to him that every time he even mentioned Zandra Stenner he was probably making Mother unhappy. Or nervous. Or sad.

"I don't think that's so," Allie defended. "Even Ferdy, and he should know about these things, thinks we're all pretty well adjusted."

"Just why should Ferdy know about these things?" I challenged.

"Because he's always reading stuff, and he knows more than you and me put together, is why," Allie said.

"If he's so smart," I said, thoroughly sick of Ferdy altogether, "why isn't he older?"

"Huh?"

One point for me.

(The best thing is that even if Allie and Ferdy should be friends for life, making us all captive to tales of Ferdy's genius forever, at a certain point I can ask almost the same thing—when he's thirty-five or forty, I mean. "If he's so smart, how come he's not younger?")

Apart from trying to keep things on an even keel,

as they say, and trying to make life a little easier and brighter for Mother, mostly what I did, in secret, was wait. There had to be a telephone call. There had to be a private meeting. There had to be an apology.

And if all this didn't happen soon, I for one promised myself that I would make life, for certain people, absolute hell!

10.

"Now, what's all this about?" asked Mr. O'Connell the following Sunday as he pushed open the front door to the apartment. "Allie's downstairs trying to explain, and no matter what he says it isn't coming through."

Tessa sat in a corner of the couch, near a window, looking at her father. Though she was silent, she felt, inside, that she was screaming. He had to know, didn't he? Surely he understood?

Mr. O'Connell stood in the doorway a moment, his tweed overcoat still buttoned, a scarlet cashmere scarf wrapped around his neck. Impatiently he was slapping one fur-lined glove against the side of his leg. "Well, honey, just what's the matter? Come on."

There were tears behind Tessa's eyes, waiting. "I just don't happen to feel like being your daughter today," she said. "That's all."

Her father laughed softly. Not unkindly. "That's pretty difficult, you know, Tessa. Turning on and off like that. Don't I even get any warning?"

"Why should you?" Tessa asked back. "We never get any."

An expression Tessa was unfamiliar with crossed her

father's face and he sighed, but only barely. He loosened the top buttons on his coat and closed the door behind him, beginning to walk across the room toward the couch. "Tessa," he said in a low voice, "Zandra's waiting for us. Tell me what's on your mind so I can try to clear it up and we can get going. Come on. Don't be bashful. Just let it all out." He sat next to her and reached out for one of her hands, but Tessa brought both her hands to her chest and held them there.

She had meant to begin quietly. She had meant to try to discuss her complaint sensibly and as an adult. She was going to, if she had to (which she had also hoped and prayed she wouldn't) explain carefully and step-by-step. Instead, before she could stop herself, she was nearly shouting.

"Everybody around here just picks and chooses when they're going to be who they say they are, and I can't stand it anymore!"

Mr. O'Connell didn't speak. He waited, for more.

"Well, just don't sit there!" Tessa shouted finally.

"Honey, I'm not sure what you want me to say. I don't honestly understand what it is *you're* saying."

"What I'm saying is very simple. Mother gets up and announces that today she's got plans and we're on our own. Which we're not. Today, one day a week, we're supposed to be your children. Terrific! Today she wants to pretend we're not, and today we have to pretend we are! It isn't fair!"

Tessa looked away, down and out the window. Her father coughed once.

"Tessa, I'm sorry," he said. "I'm afraid I'm still at sea. Are you feeling . . . abandoned, it that it?"

"That most certainly is not it!" Tessa answered quickly. "That would be a lot better. What I'm saying is that you seem to think Allie and I can just switch on whenever we're supposed to, and then off whenever you say. You walk in here once a week expecting to be a father

for five or six hours, and expecting us to be your kids
. . . only *we* have to live a whole week with you in half
a day."

"Tessa," said Mr. O'Connell, "I know this isn't ideal.
But . . . but it's what we have just now. It won't go on
forever."

"That's for damned sure!"

"Watch it, young lady," cautioned Tessa's father.

"Why didn't you tell me?" Tessa shrieked without
warning.

"Why didn't I tell you what?" asked her father, keeping his voice purposely low.

"About her! About Fran?"

Mr. O'Connell smiled, more to himself than at Tessa.
"Darling, *you're* my daughter. Don't start imagining
suddenly you're in competition."

"I'm not talking about that," Tessa snapped. "What
I'm trying to get through to you is that you cheated me.
You should have told me. First!"

"Why?"

"Why! Because I *am* your daughter, that's why. And
because I'm certainly old enough and strong enough
and sensible enough to be taken into your confidence.
It wouldn't hurt."

Without warning, Mr. O'Connell grasped Tessa's
hand and held it. "Darling, listen. I know what you're
saying, and I apologize. Really, I do. But there's something here you may not have thought of."

"What?"

"It's not very easy on me, either, right now. I mean,
introducing both of you to a new situation, to a new
family, if you will, that suddenly you're going to have
to learn to live with. Maybe I was a little bit of a coward, Tessa. Maybe I just hoped that when you met
Zandra, you'd like her so much that meeting Fran then
would just be part of the same happy surprise."

"Well, you're wrong."

"Maybe I was," allowed Mr. O'Connell with a small smile. "Still, honey, she's a very nice girl. I know you'll both be able to make adjustments and get along."

"That's not the point!" Tessa argued. "What I want to know is what other little surprises you have up your sleeve? What else am I suddenly going to be handed and told I can adjust to?"

But before her father could reply, Tessa rushed on.

"How could you do this, all of this, without even thinking once about us, about Allie and me? How could you not even call me, if you were too busy?" An unpleasant sneer accompanied Tessa's last question, but her father ignored it, waiting.

"You could have picked me up, we could have talked!" Tessa said. "You could have phoned me, or . . . or anything! Instead, all you do is just hand it to me! Don't you ever stop to think about anyone but yourself? Are you that selfish?"

"Tessa, you're edging toward some very thin ice," warned her father. "I'm perfectly happy to discuss all this with you, as long as you remember who you are, and who I am."

"Oh, that's terrific, coming from you! You only remember once a week yourself!"

"That is not true, young lady!" defended Mr. O'Connell quickly.

"Prove it!"

Mr. O'Connell dropped Tessa's hand and stood up. "I don't have to do that, Tessa," he said. "I'm your father. I'm older than you are, and I just might have a better view of what's real and right than you do."

"Ohhh, here we go," Tessa muttered. "The old older-and-wiser trick."

"Look here, Tessa," said her father angrily. "I know none of this is easy, for any of us. But you're not making it any easier. For heaven's sakes, try to be a little patient, a little understanding."

"If you're older and wiser, you do that," Tessa commanded.

Mr. O'Connell gripped one hand with the other, in front of him, and then turned suddenly away. After a moment, he faced Tessa again, composed. He was a handsome man—tall, reddish hair now turning darker and just a little gray, with good solid features and clear eyes. Tessa had always been proud of the way her father looked. For just a second now, she tried viewing him as Zandra might have done, and understood how he might have appealed to her. Though at the moment, whatever fun and excitement he might be able to offer a woman disappeared as he struggled to open to a younger woman, one without the common experiences of disappointment and anger.

"Tessa," he said, and then paused. "Tessa, I'm going to ask a favor of you."

Tessa sat immobile, waiting.

"You have to realize, sweetheart, that while your position in all this seems sort of tenuous, sort of second-thoughtish, if you will, that mine is almost exactly the same.

"O.K. I know, from your point of view it appears that I'm in charge. After all, it's your mother and I who have separated, and it's me who has been lucky enough to find another person quickly to share life with."

"Maybe you're in too much of a hurry," Tessa said.

"That's possible, but I don't think so, Tessa," said her father with a considerate smile. "Zandra and I, we . . . feel a lot of the same things, like them, feel comfortable together. The way your mother and I did years ago, only now differently."

"I'm not asking you why you got divorced," Tessa said flatly. "And I don't particularly want to hear how ideal you and Zandra are together, if you want to know."

"I'm not going to say anything like that, Tessa," answered Mr. O'Connell. "Hopefully, as time goes on,

you'll come to understand both things a little better."
He took a breath and looked almost pleadingly at his
daughter. "You have to understand, though, Tessa, that
the way things are set up now is no more satisfying to
me than it is to you. I don't like having to push a whole
week's activity and affection into one afternoon any
more than you do. It was lots more fun living with you,
honey, and getting to know you sort of by osmosis, if
you know what I mean. Even if I didn't always listen to
what you were saying at dinner each night, so much
of what you were, are, and did and felt came through
anyway. It's what a real growing together is. And now,
because of—well, the way your mother wants it, we're
all put in the position of having to hurry, once a week,
to catch up.

"I'm not blaming her," he added quickly. "Your
mother feels, and she's probably right, too, that with the
divorce, it was important for you and Allie to begin adjusting as quickly as possible to not having me around.
Not that I was forbidden you, or anything like that.
We have our differences, but not when it comes to you
both.

"What you don't realize, perhaps," continued Mr.
O'Connell, "is how upsetting and painful this all is to
me, too. To have to pretend one day a week that everything's just fine and dandy, that there isn't any tension
in our lives. It's not easy, Tessa, thinking of you and Allie
every day and not being able to see you to tell you
about it. I have to do probably just what you do:
remember. I try to remember things I see that might interest you, or places I've gone that were fun and different that you both might like, or experiences I imagine us
having that I think could be just wonderful *actually*
having. And then, on Sundays, when I see you both,
I just can't remember everything, except how much I
love you and miss you."

Mr. O'Connell turned away from Tessa for a moment and coughed quietly, lifting a gloved hand to his face. "Tessa," he said from behind the leather, "be patient. We'll all come to a happier time, together, if we all remember that we're not in this thing alone, that each of us is off-balance in a way and only trying to stay upright until we're really and truly steady."

"You're going to marry her, aren't you, regardless?" Tessa asked coolly.

"Of course I am," said her father, puzzled a little. "Zandra and I have something new and very special and we want it to grow and continue and become even richer."

"You could keep her on the side."

"Tessa O'Connell!" said her father, open-mouthed in surprise.

"Well, you did before, didn't you?"

"That, young lady, is neither true nor any of your business, and I'd advise you to watch your mouth, closely!"

Tessa stood up and shrugged. "Come on, Daddy, I *saw* you two together!"

"You couldn't have."

"At the country club. I don't mean . . . doing anything. I just mean I saw the way you looked at each other. *Before,* if you know what I mean."

Mr. O'Connell leaned against the wall and examined his daughter closely. "Tessa, I want you to know," he said slowly, "first of all that this does not concern you. Nor do I have any intention of explaining or apologizing to you. But if you're as adult as you think you are, there is one idea that perhaps you can grasp. And when I've said what it is, that's all I'm going to say. When I'm done you just keep quiet and put on your coat and come along with us. And you *will* be gracious to Zandra and to her daughter, and to me, and you *will* be a young lady of whom I can be proud."

Tessa crossed her arms beneath her breast and waited, neither nodding agreement nor consent.

"Your mother and I are no different from many millions of other people. We met and we fell in love and got married and had children. And together, though separately, we changed. We grew in different directions and maybe even at different speeds. And then we both realized that all this changing made us less happy than we were, than we might even be alone. Period. Neither one of us was out looking for 'something on the side,' as you so eloquently put it.

"As far as Zandra and myself go, whether what you suspect was happening *did* happen concerns you not at all. Nor will it ever. But it is important for you to know that Zandra and I are like other people, too, who discovered an attraction and a sense of value and excitement that we cherish, that we want to continue.

"Unfortunately, as so often happens, when we found each other, actually getting together meant that perhaps some sadness had to be inflicted on others.

"I'm not going to discuss morality with you, the rights and wrongs, the old-fashioned or the new. I just want you to know, as you will when you're older, that having an affair, if it happens, is almost never the cause of a divorce. What it is is a symptom of a fading marriage. It couldn't ever happen if the marriage in question were as strong and healthy as it should be ideally. Your mother and I were already experiencing difficulty together, were already walking on eggs, if you will, when Zandra appeared."

Mr. O'Connell paused and then started buttoning his overcoat. "Now, Tessa," he said, "if you're ready, let's go have fun, please. Please."

Tessa was unforgiving. "Not at her house."

Mr. O'Connell looked up. "Tessa, can't you understand any of this, any of it at all?"

"Of course I can," Tessa answered, turning her back

on her father and looking out the window, a fleeting image of herself on a film screen flashing across her mind. "Zandra's a slut. She's nothing more than an old-fashioned home-wrecker! And just like a man, you've been taken in!"

The spin of her body surprised her and threw her off-balance even as she turned. And the sound of her father's hand across her face seemed to register even before the pain of the blow.

When she opened her eyes, through the blur she saw her father standing away at arm's length, looking at her with something like horror or fear on his face which rapidly changed to chagrin and shame.

"My God, Tessa!" he said. "Don't make me hate myself!"

He reached out for her and enfolded her in his arms, the warmth and comfortable odor of his tweed overcoat enveloping her. But Tessa stood without yielding. "I'm so sorry, honey," said her father into her ear. "I didn't mean to do that, Tessa, really. I'm so sorry."

Tessa would not speak. Her father waited a moment and then pulled his arms away and took a step backward, looking at her expectantly. After a moment of wordless communication, her father fastened the top button of his coat and put on his glove.

"All right, Tessa," he said calmly. "Stay here if you like. Allie and I are leaving. It's up to you."

He turned and started toward the front door of the apartment. Once there, his hand on the knob, he stopped and turned. "Tessa," he said firmly, "Zandra and I are going to be married and we want you to be happy for us, and to share with us all that we find valuable and exciting. If you won't, that's up to you. But don't ever *ever* again let me hear you use words like that, about Zandra or any other person I love. Including your mother!"

Tessa stared at him and said nothing.

"If you won't let yourself understand or forgive or share, then there's absolutely nothing I can do. Be unhappy. But Tessa, remember one thing. Unhappiness shows. And it isn't pretty."

Mr. O'Connell opened the door. "If you change your mind and want to join us, take a cab and I'll pay for it when you get there."

Without saying goodbye, Tessa's father closed the door and started down the stairway. Tessa listened to his footsteps.

11.

Have you ever found yourself turning to the left when all along, even before you've taken a step, you'd planned to make a right?

Or liking something or someone you had just *known* in advance you'd hate?

Or planning to say something slowly and carefully and in total control and suddenly instead you're screaming?

That's the kind of day I was having.

Everything I'd planned disappeared. Everything I'd wanted to say, in a way, of course, I'd said, but entirely differently. All the hours I'd spent imagining Daddy's and my discussion shattered in the reality of things. Every good intention went up in smoke and was replaced by what even I admit was rather unattractive.

Still and all, even after he and Allie had driven off, I didn't feel embarrassed or angry or ashamed. O.K., so maybe I used a few different words than I had thought

I might. But the message had gotten through. That was what mattered.

If kids ever really do go through "phases," I was certainly in a peculiar one. The afternoon turned even grayer and darker than before, and drizzle started to fall—the kind that lets you know the sky is only waiting for the thermometer to dip a few more degrees so it can really unload what it's been carrying all the time: snow.

What I said about turning left when you intended to go right followed me all day long. At first I was sort of happy, being miserable. And alone. After all, in one way I was a wronged woman. It's an oddly comfortable position in which to be. You just know you're *right*. That no matter how things actually turned out, what's done is done and it all had to be just that way. No alternatives. No second thoughts.

Sure, it may hurt a little. I didn't even really blame Daddy for whacking me. After all, when men don't understand things, sometimes they do get violent. It only went to show that even he knew I was right, about Zandra, about the way he and Mom treated Allie and me. About everything.

But the hurt disappears when you get the warm glow inside that confirms what you already knew: that your own vision, your own version of things, is the accurate one, the only accurate one. You sort of martyrize yourself, if you know what I mean. Of course, you think, of course you're going to be strung up; people hate hearing truths they've secretly thought might be valid all along. It confirms their every darkest suspicion, every secret certainty that they were afraid or unwilling to admit to. And when they're confronted by these things, their first reaction is to strike out, anywhere.

Poor me, I might have said, but I didn't. I just walked around the house, sort of smiling and nodding to myself, listening to my own thoughts and agreeing with them. Being alone is not the worst thing in the world that can happen to someone.

I did think of calling Charlotte. Not so much for confirmation of what I already knew, but just to share the scene, sort of.

But I didn't. There wasn't much she could say or ask that I needed. Besides, for just a second there, I was almost sorry Daddy hadn't accidentally hurt me a little more. Nothing serious, but maybe just half a black eye. *That* would be fun—listening to Charlotte expound on the cruelty and selfishness of mankind. Still, without something like that, everything would just be words, and at the moment that wasn't satisfactory. To me, anyway.

I also toyed with the idea of taking off. Of staging a "run-away" of some kind. I had a few good minutes there imagining Mother coming home to an empty house and imagining that I was still at Zandra's. And then finding out, when Allie and Dad came back, that I wasn't. I even stood in front of the hall closet checking out heavy, warm winter coats, in case I wound up sleeping in the back of someone's parked car for the night.

But I abandoned this as too melodramatic. It was enough to have suffered, a little, in the name of righteousness.

None of which begins to explain why I absolutely and totally cracked up when Toby Bridgeman called. And I don't mean with laughter.

Which is what I started to say about turning left when all along you'd wanted to turn right.

First of all, Toby Bridgeman had never in his entire life called me before. I mean, at the best of times we'd look at each other and smile. Maybe dance together a little. What I said before. But he'd never lifted a telephone receiver and actually dialed the right number— and actually waited until I got on the line. I mean, who knows when you pick up a phone and there's no sound?

Secondly, and maybe even better or more important, he wasn't calling me to ask me to go somewhere particular, like a party or a basketball game or a movie. I mean, that's really the easy way out, isn't it? Knowing that well, sure, you're taking a girl somewhere but that you're in fact *surrounded,* either by other guys you know, or by the "public." What can go wrong *there?*

At first, I thought I was handling everything pretty well. "Oh, hi, Toby," I said, sort of offhand. Not actually pretending to be busy or anything, but certainly not sounding surprised, either.

"What's going on?" he asked. Not incredibly articulate, I decided, but endearingly simple, anyway.

"Not much," I said. "How can I help you?"

(This last is what I *love* to hear people say on phones or in stores. It's nice and inviting, and uttered with the proper emphasis and spacing between words, it can almost always sound sincere.)

"I don't know," Toby said. "I just sort of wondered what you were doing. Now, I mean. It's a pretty mean day, isn't it?"

"For anybody but Eskimos and water freaks," I glibly replied.

"The thing is—" Toby started to say and then stopped. "I mean, well, my dad has to drive over your way to see a client and I thought, I mean, if you didn't mind or anything, or if I wouldn't be disturbing you, I thought maybe I'd just stop in and visit."

"Visit?"

"Not if you're busy!" he said quickly. "I mean, if your family's around or doing something important and all, we could just . . . well, we could do it some other time."

I smiled, maternally it felt like, and I wondered for a second if Toby knew that I was smiling. "Tessa?"

"Yes," I said. "I think it would be all right, Toby. If you want to."

"Oh." I think he was just a little surprised I said yes. "Oh. Well, in that case, I'll see you in a while. O.K.?"

"O.K."

I put down the phone and sort of examined the place. Everything was fairly neat and, besides, in a place this size, there isn't a whole lot you can do to disguise any shortcomings. As for myself, after checking in the bathroom mirror, I decided there wasn't a lot I could do with myself either. At least my eyes weren't red, or anything like that. And I was still rather neatly put together just in case I had actually been forced to accompany Allie and Daddy to Zandra's. A little extra lipstick, maybe, and a quick brush-out and that was that.

I walked back into the living room and began to have the funniest thoughts. After all, what we had here was the perfect set-up. Parents away for a while. The house to ourselves. No one to bother or interrupt or surprise us.

If, that is, your mind tended to turn in those directions.

Maybe that's really why Toby called. Maybe some extrasensory perception flashed across town to him and told him a nubile virgin was unsheltered and alone and here was his big chance.

I doubted it, but just in case, I began planning ahead. I found a pack of Mother's cigarettes and put them on the coffee table in front of the couch, along with a pack of A & P matches (elegance?). It's not that I smoke, or that I even want to start or experiment. What it is is that I remember hearing someone tell someone else once that a cigarette is as good a defense as any against an overamorous boy. I mean, who's going to try to attack you when you've got a lighted torch in your hand?

Actually, I didn't really mind the prospect of Toby sort of trying, at least. I mean, that's only natural, and even if that wasn't what he really had on his mind when he called, it would be only natural for him to try to pretend it was. Boys are like that.

So I paced a while, and then sat, and then stood and walked some more, drawing "lines," deciding how much and when and where was O.K., and what was very definitely a no-no and off-limits. If you want to know, I gave not one thought to my reputation. I mean, to the idea that if I let Toby do A or B, pretty soon everyone at school would know how far he'd gotten (or how far I'd gone), and then within hours there'd be this huge line outside the door or on the telephone, all measuring against what Toby had been able to report. After all, when you haven't even got a reputation yet, what's there to protect?

Anyway, all this planning and decision-making was the mental turning left, as I've said. The real turning right couldn't have surprised me more.

Because in about twenty minutes the doorbell rang. I answered it and there stood Toby, as advertised, all bundled up in some sort of fur-collared raincoat, jeans, and boots, looking shorter than ever because of the bulk of it all. "Hi," I said, "come on in."

"Thanks," said Toby, very formally, which almost made me laugh until I tried to think what else he could have said.

He walked in and I closed the door behind him. He looked around (probably straining his ears, as well, to discover whether or not we were alone) and then he turned to face me. He started to unbutton his coat as I stood there looking at him, and I probably even had what is kindly referred to as an inscrutable smile on my face.

Toby pulled free of the raincoat and looked around shyly for some place to put it. I motioned he could just throw it anywhere, which I guess he did. Because when again he turned to look at me, and smiled, and started to say, "Well, here we are," with no warning whatsoever I was suddenly hurling myself across the room at him, sobbing and burying my head in his shoulder.

He was probably surprised.

I'm not sure how many seconds we stood that way before he finally brought his arms up to my shoulders and rather gingerly patted my back.

I was burrowing into him so and making such a racket without really understanding any of it that I wasn't even aware how tentative his gestures were, or how almost inaudible his, "There, there," and "Hey, Tessa, what's wrong?"

I pulled back after a minute, embarrassed as hell I might admit, and very quickly indeed put a few feet between us. I walked to the windows of the living room and looked out. A mixture of rain, sleet, and snow had begun to fall, making the gloomy afternoon all the darker. It was a perfect day to stay inside near a fire and hold hands. Or something.

"Let's go for a walk!" I suggested brightly, turning around and at the same time swiping at my eyes with my hand.

"Are you crazy?" Toby asked. "It's miserable outside."

"Don't be silly," I protested, reaching down for his raincoat and throwing it up at him. "It's romantic. Walking in the rain."

"Well, maybe in the spring, when it's warm or something. Today you'll probably catch pneumonia."

But I wasn't to be stopped. Toby stood in one spot watching, vainly protesting—my health, *his* health, Christmas vacation, the basketball game Saturday night

—while I dove into the hall closet for my own stuff and dressed. "Come on, Toby," I urged. "It'll be fun!"

He shook his head doubtfully but nonetheless he did put on his coat again and within seconds we were outside, walking down the driveway toward the corner of the house, mentally bracing ourselves for the gust of misery that would come at us there as we came into the open.

I will say one thing for Toby. He could have spent the whole afternoon walking with his hands in his pockets, in silence, head ducked against the elements, silently swearing at me. He didn't. After a minute to adjust, he sort of edged closer to me on the sidewalk and reached out for my hand. I felt (surprisingly!) grateful, and I smiled and let him hold it.

We walked along Ash Street, pretty much in silence except for the occasional "Watch out! the puddle" or just "Brrrr!" After a few blocks, without discussing the decision, we apparently agreed to turn and head back up on the other side.

"Tessa," Toby said, leaning toward me to be heard over the wind, "is something the matter? Something I can help you with?"

I thought about it for a minute. "Not unless you're a wizard," I decided, "and can call back words."

"What do you mean?"

"I had a little run-in with my father," I said.

"Oh," said Toby.

I nodded. "I *think* I called his fiancée a slut," I said. Toby looked at me. I imagine he was surprised.

"You're lucky to be alive," he said after a while.

"What does *that* mean?"

"Well, you can say just about anything to anybody and get away with it," Toby said seriously. "Except for that kind of thing. I mean, when somebody thinks they're in love, the last thing you want to do is call 'the object of their affections' something like that."

"You sound like Charlotte."

"Did she say the same thing?"

"Not yet, but she will."

"We're both right, you know," Toby said. "I mean, I was reading something the other day about this thing called 'sensitivity training,' you know? And what the article said was that really, the only thing that's worthwhile about it is learning that you can say almost anything to someone as long as you first make them feel terrific. You know, you tell someone how beautiful they are, or how smart, or how much you value their friendship, and then, after they've eaten that stuff up, you lay it on them. That really, there's just this one little thing about them you can't quite understand. How can anyone so perceptive or clever do whatever it is you're really trying to get them to give up?"

"For instance."

Toby put his arm over my shoulder. It was nice. Warmer, anyway.

"For instance," he said, squeezing me, bringing me closer. "Tessa, you're a beautiful, desirable young woman. And you're so intelligent that I just can't understand how you could do something so incredibly stupid as to call your new stepmother a slut. I mean, that's about the dumbest thing I ever heard of, especially for someone as perceptive and mature as you are."

"Still, it's true."

"How do you know?"

"I don't," I answered. "But a woman can sense these things."

"Sure," said Toby. His tone was total disbelief.

"Well, we can!" I defended.

We walked a while more. "O.K.," I said finally. "You're right. It was stupid."

I looked over at Toby and he grinned at me and squeezed me again against his side.

We walked still further, now in silence, standing

very close to each other when we got to a curb, and then, our feet moving identically (right with right, left with left), we crossed a street.

"You coming to the game this weekend?"

I was feeling a little better about life when he threw that one at me. "I don't know," I teased. "A game's a game."

"Sure, but after this one, we can go out if we want."

"How?" I asked. "Your father going to play chauffeur?"

Toby shook his head and smiled. "Nope," he grinned. "By Saturday I'll be sixteen and I can drive myself."

"You will?"

"Yeah."

We walked a little way. "Still, that's not such an earth-shattering event, is it? I mean, if I don't go to this game, I'll go to some other."

"I don't think I want to wait that long," said Toby.

"For what?"

"A kiss."

I want you to know I wasn't even thinking just then. All I did was stop right there, just stop dead, and turn into him. I put my arms around his shoulders and pulled him straight at me. And I kissed him.

From a distance we must have looked like two crazy, waterlogged multicolored bears.

He kissed me back.

I liked it.

A lot.

"There!" I said, backing away and turning to start walking again. "Now I don't have to sit in the bleachers all Saturday night getting worked up over whether we will or we won't."

"Will we?"

I grinned and snuggled into Toby's body. "Of course."

12.

"You said what?" Charlotte asked, nearly shrieking.

"You heard me," muttered Tessa.

"Well, you're lucky you've got legs left," Charlotte said, shaking her head in wonderment. "I mean, he could just have removed your knees altogether. I certainly would have."

"You're being incredibly helpful," Tessa said, hugging herself on the couch, watching Charlotte pace dramatically through the small living area.

"Well, I had no idea I was walking into the house of a madwoman!"

"You can walk out again, any time."

"Oh, for heaven's sake!" Charlotte sighed, hurling herself into as much of a small, compact mass as she could at the couch's other end. "There's no need for all this snotty defense mechanism," she said. "After all, what are friends for, if not to help you out of holes?"

"How do you see yourself doing that?" Tessa wondered with the slightest edge to her voice.

"Well, first of all," Charlotte answered, "you have simply *got* to stop calling people names."

"Swell."

"I'm serious!" Charlotte announced. "Even you, Tessa, *must* be able to understand that the last thing in the world that's going to help you is calling your future stepmother dumb names."

"I don't know," Tessa mused. "Snow White never tried it, but who knows, it might have saved her a lot of indigestion."

"Cute," Charlotte pronounced. "Very cute. But dumb."

Tessa stretched, looking at her hands before her. She said nothing.

"Well, what are you going to do now?" Charlotte asked.

"I don't know." Tessa shrugged. "Wait, I guess, and see what happens."

"Tessa, tell me, are you really trying to stop this whole thing? The marriage, I mean."

"If I could, I would," Tessa decided.

"Just because they've slept together?"

"Certainly not!" Tessa defended. "That has nothing to do with it."

"Then what has?"

"I don't know," Tessa said again. "I just happen to think that this is not a suitable match." She accented the last two words. "Or, if you'd rather put it another way, that *she* is not a suitable woman for my father."

"Doesn't he get to make that decision?"

"Crazed with sex, you think he can?" Tessa asked and let out a short, all-too-knowing laugh.

"How do you know he's crazed with sex?" Charlotte demanded. "Does he kiss her all the time? I mean, can't he keep his hands off? Or what?"

"For heaven's sakes, Charlotte, he's not a sex maniac! He's just . . . well, under the old spell. He doesn't rape her or anything when we're around."

"Exactly!" crowed Charlotte. "That just goes to prove my point. He's perfectly capable of making up his own mind, rationally, intelligently. He has *not* gone off the deep end."

Tessa said nothing.

Charlotte waited a moment, looking at her friend. "I think, Tessa, that maybe you had better start adjusting. To the idea, I mean. It doesn't seem likely that you're going to stop this thing."

Tessa was up and off the sofa suddenly, standing at the window. "You simply don't understand, Charlotte. Honestly! I mean, just listen a moment. A woman who could wreck someone else's marriage—just for a fling or whatever you want to call it—simply is not a woman to be trusted. Suppose she sees someone *else* she wants? What's going to stop her from starting all over again?"

"I presume her affection for your father."

"I doubt it," Tessa said quickly.

"Tessa, she wasn't *married* when she met your father. She would be, idiot, from now on. I mean, she *couldn't* just dump one guy and pick up with another like that. People don't *do* that kind of thing."

"You wouldn't. I wouldn't. My *mother* wouldn't. But Zandra just might."

"It seems to me you're banking pretty heavily on a maybe, Tessa," Charlotte said deliberately and softly. "You can't carry on like this just because *you* think something like that might happen. You can't even discuss that intelligently with your father."

"I don't see why not. All I'm trying to do is spare him pain and embarrassment later. I should think he'd be grateful I saved him from another divorce, or a moment that could really hurt him, wipe him out."

"He won't be."

"How can you be so sure?"

"Tessa, your father is no different than you or me. How often have *we* let people spare *us* that way? I bet every kid in America at one time or another has announced that it, whatever, may be a mistake, but that it's his mistake, and he's free to make it if he chooses."

"That's infantile."

"Of course. But also true. Everybody goes through that at least once."

"Listen, Charlotte, are you going to help me, or not?"

"I can't if you won't even pretend to listen to what I'm saying. If all you're going to do is get defensive and angry."

"You are just impossible!"

"So are you!" Charlotte said swiftly and with just as much impatience in her tone.

A moment of silence passed. "Truce?" Tessa asked finally.

"Truce," agreed Charlotte. "Now, what are you going to do?"

"It's very clear," announced Tessa firmly. "I'll simply have to talk to Zandra."

"And say what?" Charlotte was doubtful.

"I'm not sure, yet," Tessa admitted. "We could sort of have a dry run, couldn't we? I mean, you be Zandra, and I'll be me, and let's see what would happen."

"But it would still be make-believe."

"That's not the point!" Tessa said sharply. "At least it would give me a chance to hear what I have to say. To listen to the way I want to sound."

Charlotte sighed. "Go ahead, then."

Tessa began pacing in front of the two small windows. "O.K.," she said. "Give me a minute."

Charlotte waited patiently, expecting very little.

"O.K.," Tessa said. "Ready?"

"Ready."

Tessa inhaled rather grandly. "Zandra, I want you to know, first of all, that what I'm going to say doesn't come easily."

"I appreciate that," Charlotte replied.

"But I really do think that we can have an honest discussion, just us two. I mean, as women we probably see things in pretty much the same light, don't you think?"

"If we do see the same things," Charlotte answered.

"I know what you're going to say," Tessa imagined aloud, running quickly on. "That after all a good number of years do separate us, and you undoubtedly know more of the world than I."

"Go easy on the number of years," Charlotte advised.

"Right," Tessa agreed. "Anyway . . . Zandra—uh—"

"Terrific," Charlotte murmured.

"Give me a chance!" Tessa said angrily. She continued to walk around the room, her arms swinging at her sides until evidently she received a mental image of her own movements and suddenly stopped, taking up a semisophisticated pose near the fireplace. "Zandra, there is absolutely no reason for you to marry my father."

"There isn't?"

"No. After all, we're all adults. People *do* live together these days, you know. Marriage is virtually passé."

"Not to me, dear," Charlotte improvised.

"Seriously, what do you gain by a small piece of paper? What would you have with it you wouldn't have without it?"

"A husband." Charlotte smiled at her own simple, strong answer.

"Of course," Tessa admitted, "but what possible difference would a written agreement make to two people who were already in love and committed? Really, it's more a way of chaining you than anything else."

"I believe it's called the tie that binds," Charlotte supplied. "Besides, dear, I *want* to be your father's *wife*, not just his mistress."

"But, Zandra, that's so old-fashioned! Just in terms of Women's Lib, really. I mean, one way you'd have everything you wanted—he'd be living with you, you'd see each other all the time, you'd have all the fun and advantages of being married. But best of all, if it didn't work out—I mean, of course it would, but just in case—this way all either of you has to do is pack and step out. No angry scenes or quarrels about who gets what. It's so easy, so *civilized*."

"Marriage has a long and healthy history, as I recall, in terms of civilization," Charlotte said.

"Of course it has! I'm not saying that for some people it's not a good thing. But for you and my father—after all, you're both sort of young yet, there are years and years ahead of you. Why lock yourselves into something like this when it isn't even necessary?"

"Tessa, it is very necessary to me. I love your father. I want to live with him. I want to be his wife. I can't think of anything—barring a sudden, fatal secret disease—that could possibly change my mind."

"Zandra, you're just not being very reasonable about all this."

"Well, *I* think I am. Besides, a woman in love doesn't have to be reasonable. And even if she were, you're not offering me very much that I want instead, dear. I've been alone a long time. I didn't like it."

"Oh, come on!" Tessa laughed rudely. "You haven't been *that* alone for *that* much time! After all, you're a big, strong, healthy woman with urges and desires and—"

Charlotte stood up, seeming very tall and stern suddenly. "Tessa, I would decide to change my tack if I were you."

"But why?" Tessa objected. "Certainly we can be honest about these things, Zandra. I mean, women do —well—need—things—every so often."

"I'm not going to argue about it, Tessa. I *do* think, though, that perhaps you'd better just settle down a little and relax into this. There is nothing that's going to keep your father and me from getting married."

The two girls stood face to face, glaring at each other, for a long moment entirely wrapped in their new personalities.

The doorbell shattered their intensity.

"Oh, my God!" Charlotte said, blinking. "Who's that?"

Tessa shrugged. "Probably United Fund or the Red Cross or something. Everyone we *know* comes right up the stairs and knocks on the door."

She turned away from Charlotte and went to the front door of the apartment, snapping on the landing light before she opened the door and poked her head out into the hallway. "Who is it?" she called.

"Zandra Stenner," was the reply. "May I come up?"

Before Tessa could reply, Zandra opened the storm door below and stepped from the darkness into the lighted stairway. As she began to climb the stairs, Charlotte became a whirlwind of activity—grabbing for her raincoat, her scarf and purse.

"I'm getting out of here!" she whispered to Tessa as she threw on her coat.

"Don't you dare!" Tessa whispered back. "I *need* you! You've got to stay!"

"Nope, this is your show, Tessa. There's nothing I can do." Charlotte hugged Tessa briefly at the doorway. "Call me later, O.K.?"

Tessa didn't answer, feeling small and unprepared and deserted and angry simultaneously.

"Oh!" Zandra exclaimed as Charlotte stepped out onto the landing. "I didn't know Tessa had friends in. Please, won't you stay?"

"I can't," Charlotte said weakly, stepping past Zandra and running down the stairs.

Zandra Stenner entered the living room as the door below drifted noisily back onto its catch. "I'm sorry, Tessa. I didn't mean to barge in like this."

Tessa shrugged and took up a position at the windows. "It's O.K.," she answered sullenly. "Charlotte was about to go anyway."

"Well, then, I feel better," Zandra said cheerfully. "Gosh, what a miserable night it's going to be. It must be below freezing already." She shivered to demonstrate and began unwrapping her fur-lined raincoat. "You wouldn't have a cup of tea about, would you, Tessa? I'm absolutely chilled through and through."

"Where's Dad?"

Zandra smiled, dropping her coat on a corner of the couch. "I sent him and Allie off to an early movie," she said pleasantly. "I thought this might be a good time for us to have a little chat."

"Oh."

"If you don't mind."

"Why should I mind?" Tessa asked. "It's probably a good idea." She pushed herself off the wall near the windows and went toward the kitchen. "You could have coffee, instant, if you wanted. The only tea we have is iced. Mix."

"Coffee would be fine," Zandra said. "Well, this is really very nice, isn't it?" she added conversationally as Tessa put a kettle beneath a faucet and turned on the tap. "Really, it's quite cozy and snug and warm."

Tessa said nothing, standing in the open kitchen with her back to Zandra Stenner, her mind awhirl with things to say, questions to ask, demands to make. Nerves kept her entirely mute.

"Your father told me about your talk this morning, Tessa," Zandra said with no more preamble.

Tessa dropped a carefully measured teaspoonful of instant coffee into a mug.

"Tessa, I'm not a terrible person, you know."

"Sugar, or milk, or anything?" Tessa asked in a dead tone over her shoulder.

"Sugar. One," said Zandra. "Tessa, you can't possibly even begin to know me well enough to dislike me. Unless," and Zandra let herself laugh a little in a friendly, modest way, "you're like Dr. Fell and know not well why but nonetheless, you do. Do you?"

"I don't know what you mean," Tessa said, turning finally and holding out the coffee to Zandra.

"You know, that wonderful old rhyme," Zandra explained, taking the mug from Tessa's outstretched grip. "Something about 'I cannot tell you why too well, or whatever, I only know I do not like you, Dr. Fell.' I can't remember the way it actually goes, but it's something like that."

"Oh," said Tessa noncommittally, leaning against the kitchen counter, crossing her arms beneath her breast and not smiling in return.

"Won't you come in and sit down with me, Tessa?" Zandra suggested. "I mean, we're not in a prize ring or anything, are we? Can't we try to understand each other?"

Tessa shrugged and moved back into the living room. She selected a single chair instead of the couch and sat down, facing Zandra, who had picked the couch.

"Now," Zandra began, smiling encouragingly, "why don't you just tell me exactly why you don't like me?"

"I never said that."

"Then tell me why you object to your father marrying me."

"Because—" Tessa started, "because of the way you did it."

"Did what, dear?"

"Stole him."

Zandra sipped from her coffee a moment. "Tessa, I didn't steal him. I didn't help break apart your parents' marriage."

"Sure," Tessa said dully. "Whatever you say."

"All right, Tessa, in a way I *will* accept some responsibility. Because of me, your father at least had an alternative in mind. But even if I hadn't been around, believe me, dear, I don't honestly feel he would have stayed much longer with your mother anyway."

"You couldn't know," Tessa said.

"I don't, not for sure," Zandra agreed. "But it's the feeling I get. From talking with your father."

"You don't call coming on like some starving streetwalker in public being responsible?"

"You mean, I presume, like a whore?" Zandra said evenly.

"That's fine with me," Tessa said meanly. "Your word, not mine."

"And just where am I supposed to have . . . solicited?"

"Oh, come on!" Tessa said angrily, standing up. "I saw you! I saw you both!"

"Tessa, just what exactly are you referring to?"

"At the country club. Last Christmas, for Pete's sake!"

Zandra seemed to think back a moment. "Tessa, for your information, your father and I never even began going out until sometime in February."

"Don't tell me that! I saw you!"

"What on earth did you *see?*"

"The way you two looked at each other. The kind of looks you were sending each other. The little touch-and-feel game you played."

Zandra smiled, faintly. Not unkindly. "Tessa, dear, older people sometime, socially I mean, do make contact physically. We can talk and touch someone in a friendly, gracious way and not be falling over in heat."

"You know what really surprised me?" Tessa asked suddenly. "That my mother was there, through it all, and never even noticed."

"Tessa, there wasn't anything to notice. When I met your father, I *also* met your mother. I've never made a practice of luring other women's men into my clutches."

"I'll bet," Tessa said under her breath.

"Tessa, when I met your father, *if* you'll recall, I wasn't just a single lady roaming the room. I was there with someone, too. And for all I knew at the time, your father was a perfectly happily married man. To be sure, I thought he was attractive and virile. But whether you believe it or not, I do have some standards."

"Oh sure," Tessa said. "They all have to be at least six feet tall."

Zandra smiled, more to herself than at Tessa. "Tessa, listen. There just isn't any way you can provoke me. No matter how you try, believe me. One of us at least knows what's at stake here. And I have no intention of losing it."

"I'm not trying to *provoke* you," Tessa answered quickly. "I'm telling you exactly what I said to Daddy. That you're not a nice woman. That if it's just sex, fine, have it, but don't make it legal."

"But why shouldn't he?" Zandra asked. "Why would you want your own father to live that way?"

"He can live any way he wants, as far as I'm concerned, only not with you."

"Why, Tessa? Just tell me why?"

"All right!" Tessa shouted. "Because there's no way of knowing, of being sure of you, that's why. If you did this once, to him and my mother, what's to keep you from doing it again, with someone else? How could he ever be sure of you? Be sure you really meant whatever you tell him when he already *knows* what kind of woman you are. It's simple common sense."

"That it is," Zandra said firmly. "Simple. And common."

"So are you!"

"No, Tessa, I'm not," Zandra said, reining in her own anger. She took a deep breath. "You don't mind if I have a cigarette, do you?" she asked, opening her handbag and pulling out a package of cigarettes and a gold lighter.

Tessa didn't answer. She watched Zandra snap the lighter into flame and inhale. There was a grim smile on Tessa's face, almost an "I-told-you-so" look. She felt very tall and very strong and very much in charge of the scene.

Zandra blew out the smoke she had held a fraction of a second in her lungs. "You seem to think that divorce makes a wicked woman out of everyone."

"It certainly can," Tessa answered, emphasizing the last word.

"Of your mother, for instance?"

"Leave her out of this!" Tessa said hotly. "My mother has nothing to do with this."

"Well," Zandra said, leaning back on the couch, "at least now we're beginning to get somewhere. You're quite right, dear, she hasn't. She's a fine woman, and clearly a wonderful mother to have such loyalty in her children."

Tessa didn't think it worthwhile to say anything.

"Tessa, why don't you think people deserve whatever happiness they can find?"

"I'm not talking about happiness," Tessa complained. "I'm talking about—about breaking up marriages for your own reasons."

"Just what kind of life do you think I lead, dear?" Zandra asked. "I'm hardly a *femme fatale,* trapping men and making them give me expensive gifts."

"You tell me!" Tessa said demandingly. "You're certainly not going to pretend that my father is the *first!*"

Zandra did not flinch. "No, I wouldn't do that. He's not."

Tessa smiled triumphantly.

"I don't blame your husband," Tessa said, speaking very slowly, accenting each word, knowing in advance the power of her own thought and the pain it could produce. "He must have gone through hell with you."

"How do you mean?" Zandra asked almost as carefully.

Tessa did not hesitate. "Sleeping around. Boy, if I'd been him, I'd have made you pay through the nose."

Zandra's expression changed perceptibly, but Tessa could not quite understand why. The half-smile on Zandra's lips seemed to tell Tessa that the balance of power had just shifted, but Tessa couldn't begin to fathom how it had, or why.

"My husband, dear," Zandra said evenly, "died, quite suddenly, when he was very young. When we both were very young. Even before Bunch was born."

Tessa stared at Zandra Stenner, amazed and now, suddenly, afraid.

"It was all so meaningless," Zandra provided. "It might interest you to know, dear, that he and I were very much in love. That, old-fashioned as this sounds to you, we had both been . . . virginal when we married. And that for many years afterward, after the accident, I was painfully faithful to my memories, to my love for him."

"How?" Tessa managed. "I mean, what happened?"

"It doesn't really matter, does it, dear?" Zandra asked. "It happened, that's all, on a rainy night and on a slippery road." Zandra smiled warmly and shook her head a little. "You see, Tessa. Reallly, I didn't drive him away. Nor would I ever have done."

Tessa was furious, at herself, at Zandra. She spun around and faced the windows, covered now with droplets of a cool rain. She held herself in, refusing to let herself soften or weaken. It didn't make any difference, what Zandra told her. That had nothing to do with *now,* with her *father.*

"Tessa," Zandra called softly. "Come on. Sit down, here near me."

Tessa turned and sat on the edge of the couch.

"Now, look, dear," Zandra said. "I want to be as

honest with you as I can. As you'll let me be. All right?"

"What?" Tessa said, not looking at Mrs. Stenner.

"Just this," Zandra said, starting to reach out a hand toward Tessa and then seeming to change her mind, knowing in advance perhaps that Tessa would pull back, would object. "It is true that in these last ten years, say, I haven't been exactly holding myself off from men. But I'm not about to feel guilty for that, Tessa. Realistically, honestly, Tessa, do you want me to have no satisfaction, of any kind?"

Tessa didn't know how to answer.

"Darling, listen," Zandra continued after a moment, "I'm not admitting to your worst fears. I haven't been, I wasn't ever promiscuous. Truly I wasn't. As a matter of fact, I've been an incredibly fortunate woman. I've met and known some truly wonderful men, people who were open and honest and intelligent. Not hundreds, dear. I'm sorry to disappoint you. But my life has happily been filled from time to time with caring for, and being cared about. That's a very nice, and very normal, sense of warmth and gratitude to have, believe me."

"Then you don't even need Daddy," Tessa said in defense. "I mean, if all that's true, surely there's someone else who would do just as well."

Zandra at last did reach out a hand toward one of Tessa's, and when she caught it, she held it firmly. "But we're not mentioning love, Tessa. Love. It's here, dear, really. I love your father. Miraculously, he loves me. I'm still a lucky lady, don't you see, and I want so much to stay that way." Zandra paused, lowering her voice. "Darling, I think your father feels lucky, too. I want him to. And I want him always to feel that way, always."

Tessa's shoulders had rounded, sunk just a little perceptibly. From a distance, one might have thought her bested now.

Zandra let go of Tessa's hand and pushed out her cigarette. "Tessa, I don't expect you to like me just because your father and I are going to be married. I expect to have to earn your affection, your respect. Just let me try, at least, will you? I don't think that's asking for too much, do you?"

Tessa examined her hands as Zandra stood up and wrapped her coat about her body.

For a moment, Tessa was conscious of Zandra standing nearby, not moving. She still did not look up.

"Tessa," Zandra said finally, "I won't bore you with asking to be your friend. But if it does happen, darling, I mean if in spite of yourself it happens, don't fight it. We could all have such a good time together."

Zandra picked up her purse from the couch and walked around the sofa toward the front door of the apartment. There, she stopped a moment and looked back at Tessa's motionless figure. She smiled to herself and leaned over to a small, thin table and snapped on a tiny pewter lamp.

Then she opened the door and left, closing it so quietly behind her that Tessa was scarcely able to hear it catch.

13.

I can't tell you what was going through my mind. Not exactly, not precisely, not consecutively. One thing: I remember telling myself, "Oh no, you're not going to be taken in by anything as soapy as that!"

I know I wasn't conscious of deciding that I hadn't yet given up.

At one moment, though, I do remember wondering where my mother was.

And then feeling deserted. Not suddenly, but instead all along. Alone. Even Charlotte had skipped out when she should have stayed. Not for me, particularly, but for the sake of our friendship.

Night was outside. I felt isolated. The lamp that Zandra had switched on was the only light in the room. I felt cold. I could hear the rain against the windows, pushed up noisily by gusts of wind that almost frightened me because they seemed so vicious, so revengeful.

I bucked myself up, sort of, by recognizing paranoia when I saw it. The wind wasn't avenging. It wasn't directed only at me. After all, even then I knew that if you can laugh at something, you haven't gone round the bend entirely.

I felt suddenly hungry and staggered into the kitchen. I opened the door of our refrigerator. Bleak, bleak, bleak. A couple of obviously past-it apples; a few slices of Swiss cheese in Saran wrap. A bottle of half-spent club soda. Butter. Sour cream.

I wondered what Mother thought Allie and I were supposed to eat for breakfast tomorrow, before heading off to school.

Then, without really thinking what I was doing, I was putting on my warmest coat, wrapping a scarf around my neck, and booting up. I grabbed an umbrella from the front closet and only at the door turned back and made a dash to the refrigerator. How bad can an apple get?

I stuffed the cheese into a pocket and put the apples into another. Then I was back at the door and opening it and heading down the steps toward the darkness.

When I got outside, I really hadn't figured exactly

what I was meaning to do. It didn't make a difference, actually, one direction or the other. For a moment I thought about heading toward the bus stop on Colorado and riding downtown for a visit to my little angel. And then I knew the museum probably would be closed, and that she and I would just have to communicate telepathically. But not yet.

I decided, unconsciously I think, to stay off the main thoroughfares. Maybe I even felt a little like some midnight felon, creeping through neighborhoods undetected, trying to spot a likely house to enter. Though I wasn't looking for a house at all.

I started walking, very quickly, fighting the wind and the rain, and deliberately moving away from any route either my mother or my father, with Allie, would take home. I didn't want a pair of headlights picking me out in the darkness.

I can be very rational about all this now. Trying to figure out what I did and why. But then, that night, almost everything I did was instinctive. At the best, I might have said aloud, "Well, which?" Or "What now? Where?" But that was about it. Any kind of thought that led to my own muttering was deeply buried and without words or images of any kind.

One thing: I wasn't thinking about Zandra and what she had said. As far as Zandra went, I didn't want to think about her at all.

But what did sort of keep me warm and cozy as I sloshed along was the idea that everyone would be sorry. That they'd all be frantic with worry. Probably even call the police. The Bureau of Missing Persons, if such a thing really exists. And they'd be up all night, drinking coffee and making phone calls, blaming each other, arguing. The arguing appealed to me, a lot.

I don't know how far I'd gone, or how long I'd been gone, when I must have decided I was quite far enough away. I remember that the first car I tried to get into was locked. And that the window on its right was open just a little at the top. I tried to slip my hand and arm inside to pull up the latch, but I couldn't.

I wasn't angry. I figured only that it would take me a little while longer, that was all. So I just kept walking. And after a while, the rain began to seem almost friendly. The sound of my own footsteps on the slippery sidewalks had a rhythm of its own, and I fell in with it in my mind, rhyming nonsense things as I walked, sort of humming and half singsonging as I crossed streets and stopped at alleys to look for refuge.

I don't know what street it was, but I stopped finally and looked up at a dark, old sort of Victorian house. It was totally still, standing there tall and turreted in the dark, the wind and rain circling the house as though they were looking for that one little chink through which to enter.

There was a flagstoned driveway running up along the house and I started to follow it back. There, behind the house, was a wooden, equally old-fashioned garage (maybe it was a carriage house). A tiny and very fragile-looking walkway led from the back of the house to the garage, not really much good in bad weather, almost halfhearted about its supposed purpose.

The back yard was surrounded by fencing and some sort of trees or bushes that had turned brown before emptying their foliage. The neighbors' houses were hidden behind these. No one could see me if I tried to get into the garage. Which I did, through a small door on the side of the building which pulled open finally after a lot of heaving and heavy breathing.

Inside was a car, and a lot of dirt. The building was big enough, I guess, for maybe three cars. The one that stood so forlorn and dust-covered was white, though it wasn't easy to tell. I walked around it first, just sort of feeling its sides. Above one wheel was a little silver sign: "Packard." I'd never even heard of this kind of car before, so you know how old it had to be.

But, bless it! The car was open.

I pulled open a back door and eased in backward, my legs still dangling outside. Then I got out very quickly and pulled off my raincoat and shook it out, otherwise I'd get the back seat absolutely drenched.

I eased back in and just sat there a moment, on the edge of the seat, looking out into the dark building. I didn't for a minute think about scary things like rats or burglars or bats. I couldn't look too closely at things because it was so dark, but I didn't really need to. I'd found what I had set out to, and the wind outside made me feel quite accomplished and grown-up, since after all I was inside, warm, and eventually dry.

I did have one bad moment, right at first. Suppose someone came into the garage to start the car. Suppose I had fallen asleep. Suppose they didn't even bother to look in the backseat, since they weren't expecting anything there anyway. Suppose they started the car and drove off. Suppose I was kidnapped!

Which is a totally dumb idea. A stowaway just doesn't try to blame someone else.

I guess I'd gotten hungry finally, for I crammed a couple of slices of cheese into my mouth, and then washed them down with one of my apples.

Actually, I felt rather secure, sitting there with the wind and rain pelting down outside, rattling the sides of the small building. I pulled up my feet (boots off) and covered the lower half of my body with my raincoat and almost snuggled there, hugging myself, and feeling quite comfortable.

I didn't consciously start to think about things. More, it was like those nights everyone has when they're absolutely beat and fall into bed certain they'll pass out in seconds—but don't. Some little thought or worry surfaces, and there you are, stuck for hours, as

one idea or vision comes after the other and there's no
way to stop. You just know that the night is a lost one,
and sooner or later you have to relax into it, reminding
yourself all the while that even if you're not sleeping,
still and all your body is resting and that the next day,
while your eyes may fall out, nonetheless you can still
get through whatever's coming and make it back home.
To try again.

Anyway, my head did start its own little waltz. One
idea whirling and whirling and then being passed on to
another "partner," who held it gently a second before
reversing its spin and sending it reeling toward some
totally different idea.

I remember giving points to Zandra for at least
being honest. About her past, I mean. I wasn't ready,
quite, to believe that a few fellows along the way were
the whole bundle, but at least she had admitted experiences. This did not, however, change my own mind
about whether she and Daddy were suitable or not.
After all, who wants their father involved with a scarlet woman?

That idea ran right onto the next: what about my
own mother? I don't mean when she and Daddy were
married. I mean then, that minute, right now. For
example, I had absolutely no idea at all where she
was all day long. Suppose it wasn't just another meeting
of the Greater Park Hill Committee? Suppose she had a
secret lover. Suppose that after Christmas she would sit
Allie and me down and tell us exactly what Daddy was
telling us. That there were some changes being made.

I dismissed this idea purposely and rather angrily.
Surely I would know in advance, I decided. After all,
I'd seen the heated expressions on Daddy and Zandra's
faces. Surely I would be able to read the signposts of
my very own mother's emotional crises. And, as far as
I could tell, there weren't any.

But suppose she were to have some, in the future?

Suppose, like Zandra, Mother met first one very nice man and then maybe another. Really O.K. guys that she knew she didn't want to marry, but who were fun to be with and generous and loving. Is it right to force someone to give up being a human being just because she has responsibilities, like Allie and me?

Again, I remember, I pushed this consideration away by deciding that one's responsibilities came first, period. That after you had made sure you had supported and helped and fed and nourished your own, then—maybe—you could open yourself up to others. But not before.

(Anyway, that's the way I would live.)

I think, pretty soon, I began to feel sorry for myself. I also think I recognized this and cleverly (crazy people are like this, I'm told) I decided that I wasn't feeling sorry only for myself, that Allie came in there somewhere, too, and that if no one else cared about him and his feelings, I certainly did. (I chose to ignore the obvious: that Allie was perfectly happy going along with whatever anyone else decided to do as long as it was fun, or seemed to be, and different.)

After a while, I guess, everything got all jumbled up. I mean, Toby floated through my mind once, and I'm sure that Fran Stenner herself crossed the landscape, too, and maybe even Charlotte. But the darkness of the garage, and my own hugging myself and the noise of the storm outside—everything combined to form a soft, comforting backdrop finally and I fell asleep, just like that, sitting up (although during the night I relaxed and slid down to lie across the seat) in the back of a borrowed and hopefully forgotten car in the garage of someone I didn't know.

I didn't dream. Anything. Which just goes to show you how severe an emotional stress I had been under.

But I awoke very, very early. It was hardly light. The weather had improved, at least as far as I could tell from the back seat: no rain assaulted the tiny building, and the wind, if there was any, had gotten quite gentle.

I opened the car door and stretched my legs. I was starving! I remembered the apple I had left and really wolfed it down as though I were some sort of prisoner of war at my first meal in months. I combed my hair a little, although there really wasn't any need. I looked into the building and saw, for the first time, stacks and stacks of ancient wooden picture frames and storage boxes and, in one corner, almost a whole toolshed of equipment leaning against the wall.

I wasn't in any real hurry to leave my hideout. Mostly because it was cold outside (I could tell that because, even in the garage, now I could see my own breath) and, way down deep, because I was suddenly very nervous. About going home.

I huddled in the back seat a while, waiting for the sun to come up a little more. And then, finally, I knew I had to leave.

I was very careful about my departure. After all, I didn't want some man, up early and getting ready to leave for his job, looking out a back window and seeing this mysterious figure emerge from an abandoned building. I checked first, before leaving the garage, standing in its tiny doorway, looking around, listening for sounds of people or stray dogs. After a minute of waiting, since everything seemed quiet and probably still sleeping, I slipped out of the garage and closed its door behind me and walked very softly and quickly up the driveway toward the street.

It took me a few moments to figure out where I was. Everything was incredibly clear, after the storm. The air, the sunshine, the colors of the brown-green winter lawns with just the hint of yesterday's snowflakes sitting in washed-out little piles under a few tall, spreading trees: everything was really dazzling. I stood on the sidewalk in front of my unknown host's house looking up, feeling suddenly very glad that it had been night and pitch dark when I decided to linger there overnight. The house's upper windows were broken and badly patched with cardboard. The paint along the ridges of the roof was peeled and chipped. The lawn hadn't been seen to in months, I could tell. A pile of forgotten newspapers had collected on the front porch. With a shudder I realized they could have been (and perhaps had already been) an invitation to burglars, or to people like me, squatters, who needed shelter.

Realizing then how lucky I really had been to have survived the night, I figured out where I was and in what direction I had to go, and started off.

Pretty soon I wasn't just sauntering along. Apart from the chill in the air, I realized with a really uncomfortable sensation that I had to go to the john.

I never even saw the car. I was too intent on my interior problem, and cursing myself for not having the good sense to hide out in a different kind of neighborhood, one where there might have been a donut shop or at the very least a gas station.

Besides that, I wouldn't have recognized the car even if I had seen it. Because it was Zandra's.

14.

"There!" Fran pointed suddenly, turning quickly toward her mother. "Over there, on the corner."

Zandra put her right foot quickly on the brake and slowed the car. "Are you sure?" she asked.

"No," Fran said. "It's hard. She's all bundled up. But I think so."

Zandra snapped on her turn signal and made a U-turn, bringing her car easily in line again and driving slowly toward the figure that stood wrapped warmly and half-hidden in her heavy clothes on the corner. Fran rolled down her window. "Tessa?" she called, as the car eased along the curb. "Tessa?"

Tessa already had one foot off the curb, starting for the opposite side of the street. She stopped, nearly fell into the gutter, and turned to see who had called her name. She didn't answer the call. She stood finally balanced again, staring at the car.

Fran Stenner smiled a little nervously and opened her door. "Come on," she urged. "You must be frozen."

Tessa stood a moment more, perhaps debating with herself, before she nodded at her own decision, and at the invitation.

She was silently grateful for the heat of the car.

"Where to?" Zandra asked her gently, leaning across Fran before starting the car again in a slow progress. "Your house or ours?"

"I don't care," Tessa said.

Zandra nodded and faced ahead, looking at the roadway as she drove. "You've given us all quite a scare, Tessa," she said after a moment.

Fran brightened and a broad smile faced Tessa. "One thing, anyway, kid," she said. "At least there's no school for us today. I mean, how could any teacher expect us to show up in the midst of all this *Sturm und Drang?*"

Tessa was unforgiving and refused to ask what exactly that meant. It was just like Fran to try to overpower you with some sort of weird expression like that.

"Tessa," Zandra said, "your father's at my house. Your mother's with Allie at home. You have to tell me where you want to go."

"And the police are all over the city!" Fran said eagerly.

"Good," Tessa mumbled. "I'm glad."

"Is it in your mind, Tessa," asked Zandra slowly, turning the car, "to do something like this every so often? Or is this it? I just want to know what to expect."

"Very funny," Tessa said in a quiet voice.

"No, it really isn't," Zandra argued quickly. "What you've done is mean and unforgivable, as far as I'm concerned. You've given your parents one hell of a scare and one hell of a bad night. I hope you're quite proud of that."

Tessa did not answer. She stared out the windshield at the roadway.

"If you were mine," Zandra said almost under her breath, "I'd whale the tar out of you."

"But I'm not," Tessa said with some satisfaction.

Zandra pulled the car into a gas station and turned its ignition off. "I'll just be a minute," she announced, opening her door.

Tessa and Fran sat silently, watching Zandra walk toward a phone booth at the corner of the station.

"Where *were* you?" Fran asked.

"Just out," Tessa said.

"It really *wasn't* very nice, you know," Fran said.

"I don't care," Tessa answered. "I felt I needed it, and I did it. And that's all I have to say."

"Tessa, listen," Fran said. "I mean, I know we're not best friends or anything, but can I say something?"

"Who could stop you?"

Fran smiled. "That's not terribly gracious."

Tessa shrugged.

"Tessa, my mother is a very nice person, really."

"Of course you think so."

"You know, you can't stop them."

"I don't know that."

"I do," Fran said firmly. "And secretly, I think you do, too."

Tessa sat without speaking.

"Short of killing yourself, what can you do?" Fran wanted to know. "And even then, all you'd do is delay things a while. Come on. Give in."

"Never."

Zandra slipped back into the driver's seat. "All right. I made your decision for you. We'll go see your father."

She started the car and pulled into the traffic. "By the time we get home," she said to neither girl in particular, "at least the police will be able to relax. God! I hate making people worry and stay up all night for nothing!"

Tessa straightened. "Nothing!" she said loudly. "It may be nothing to you, but not to my father!"

"Don't expect to be welcomed like the prodigal, dear," Zandra said. "Relief generally gives way to anger at moments like this."

"Well, I'm pretty mad myself, if you want to know!"

Tessa's head snapped back, facing forward, and she felt suddenly very hot. And suddenly very uncomfortable. Secretly, she decided, she was glad she would be facing her father instead of her mother. She had a few things she wanted to say to him.

Zandra's car nearly skidded as it swung into her driveway. Before Tessa could even open her door, her father had come out the front door of Zandra's house and was running across the lawn.

He reached into the front seat and pulled Tessa out with a rough urgency that melted as he hugged her for a long moment. He did not speak. Tessa half-expected him to let her go and then, just maybe (if Zandra was right), slap her hard across the face.

But Mr. O'Connell just held on a moment more before he half-released her and started to guide her into the warm house.

Once inside, Fran excused herself and went into the kitchen. Tessa was guided into the library by her father.

"Are you freezing, sweetheart?" he asked solicitiously. He took her coat and scarf from her and threw them on the couch. Then he walked to the fireplace and bent down, turning a gas jet up until the flames in the brick jumped higher and a new warmth flooded the space.

Tessa sat on the couch, staring at the fire. Zandra came into the room and stood by Mr. O'Connell. There was silence but for the slight noises the fire made.

Mr. O'Connell coughed. "Tessa," he said, "your mother wants to know if you want her to come over here."

"No," Tessa answered lifelessly.

"She's sent Allie ahead to school," Mr. O'Connell added.

Tessa just nodded.

"I'm not going to scold you, Tessa," said her father.

Tessa said nothing. She shrugged after a minute, sending the gesture out into the silent room where it seemed to her to echo. Everything seemed to be moving so slowly.

"I don't know what went on in your mind," Mr. O'Connell said after a moment. "But you've made us very, very unhappy, Tessa. And frightened, for you."

"I'm fine," Tessa allowed in a monotone.

"I'm glad of that," said her father. "And so is your mother. And so are the police."

"I'm not going to feel guilty," Tessa announced.

"No, I don't expect you will," agreed her father. "I just want you to know two things, Tessa. First, I'm awfully grateful you're O.K. That we have you back, safe and sound. And second, darling, listen very carefully. We know how you feel, Zandra and I. And we're sorry if you can't agree to let us try to find our own happiness. But we're going to, Tessa. We want you to share it with us. That invitation's still open. But if you can't, none-theless we're going to try to find it ourselves."

Mr. O'Connell walked across the small room and leaned down to kiss Tessa's hair. "Give us a chance, sweetheart," he said as he straightened up.

As he started to leave the room, Tessa came to life. "Is that all you're going to say?" she asked angrily.

Mr. O'Connell stopped on the threshold as Fran came into view behind him. "Yes, Tessa. I don't know what else I *can* say."

"Don't you want to hear what *I* think? Don't you want to know what *I* have to say?" Tessa asked with an edge of disbelief now in her voice.

"Darling, I think I already know how you feel. There really isn't anything else to say, is there, except that we love you and we want you to be happy if you can."

Tessa sat open-mouthed, staring at her father. Mr. O'Connell turned to look at Zandra. "I've got to get to the office," he said. "I'll call you from there."

Zandra nodded.

"Now wait!" Tessa commanded at the top of her lungs, standing up. "Wait!"

But her father's progress to the front hall closet and then out the front door was uninterrupted.

Tessa stood, impotent, in the library. After a second, she turned to face Zandra, her mouth open to speak. Bur Zandra spoke first, a smile on her face that stopped Tessa's anger. "Darling," she said, "I'm not your dis-ciplinarian. I only want to be your friend."

Saying no more, Zandra Stenner left the room, still with a smile.

Fran took a step into the library. "Hell, isn't it?" she said lightly. "I mean, not having anyone left to fight with."

Tessa sank unhappily back down onto the couch. Fran turned and seemed to leave the room but returned within a second carrying a small tray she must have left on a table just outside the door in the living room. "I thought you might need something like this," she said, putting the tray on a coffee table before Tessa. The aroma of hot chocolate steamed toward Tessa's nose from the two mugs on the tray.

Fran bent down and picked up one, sipping at it and then holding it, standing before Tessa. "Do you want a bath?" she asked. "Shall I ask for breakfast?"

Tessa shook her head dispiritedly. She reached for her own mug and took a swallow. "No one seems to care," she said, putting her hands around the porcelain for its warmth.

"Everyone cares," Fran said. "Even me."

The question mark on Tessa's face made Fran laugh, just a little. "Yes, I do, too," she said, "in my own silly way and for my own silly reasons." She reddened.

Tessa was uncertain what to say. She didn't want to ask how or why. That was too much like begging.

"Not so much about you, I admit," Fran added suddenly. "But I certainly do care about myself."

"I don't see how this would change things for *you*," Tessa said.

"It does, though, just as much as it does for you," Fran argued. "Of course, we're both nearly old enough so that we're not going to suffer any severe traumas."

Tessa frowned. "So you say."

"Oh, really, Tessa!" Fran smiled. "Come on. After all, it's not as though you needed to have your father around all the time. What point is there in growing up if we don't grow up independent, too?"

"You don't understand," Tessa replied. "I love my father."

"O.K.," Fran said lightly. "But look ahead a little, just for a minute. Almost every day, from now on, you're going to be on your own. You're going to *want* to be on your own. Kids grow up and move out. You'll always have him, when you need him. But it seems to me you won't be admitting that you need him quite so often anymore. Not just you. Any of us."

"Look, I for one am not about to abandon my family."

"You're deliberately misunderstanding," Fran said. "Let me try again. Look, Tessa, you've had him for fourteen years. Let us have him for just a little while, before it's too late."

Tessa smiled. "That doesn't make any sense at all. If I'm supposed to be old enough to do without, and you're even older, what do you need him *for?*"

Fran scowled. "I've never had a father, Tessa."

"You seem to have weathered O.K."

"On the outside," Fran admitted. "But I've never had what you or almost any of the kids we know had: a father *every* day. I mean, you get so used to having him around you can almost ignore him. *I* never got to do that." Fran paused and reached for her own mug, which she carried to the fireplace. "I'm not saying my mother hasn't been simply terrific, understand. But, when you get right down to it, I just never had the same kind of affection and support you had."

"No doubt that's why you throw yourself at boys," Tessa injected sharply. "It's not very becoming."

"And that's not very fair," Fran answered quickly. "I'm not terrifically interested in your own version of my psyche, you know."

"But I bet I'm right," Tessa persisted. "You're just auditioning boys to play father."

Fran turned away from Tessa and stared into the fireplace, sipping her hot chocolate. "Amateur psychologist," she muttered.

"But accurate," Tessa rejoined.

Fran turned quickly. "Look, let's get something straight. I want my mother to marry your father. I want to have your father around, every day. I want to be able to come home and tell him things, or ask him things. I want to be part of a real family, even if mostly it's all make-believe."

"You don't have to have *my* father to do that," Tessa objected. "Even your mother admits he's not the first man she's been with all these years."

"She's a normal, healthy woman, Tessa O'Connell, and there isn't any way you can make me, or her, embarrassed about that."

Tessa put down her mug and stood. "Listen, Fran. I'm not mad at you. Or really at your mother. I just happen to think—I *know*—this whole thing is a mistake. I'm only trying to stop it." Tessa shrugged. "It's nothing personal."

"But it *is* selfish!"

"You'll have another chance," Tessa said. "Your mom doesn't look like the moss-gathering type."

"I'm not talking about me!" Fran objected. "I'm talking about *you!* Trying to keep two people from doing what *they* want because you happen to be against it! You can't just go around making other people act the way you think they should!"

"Gracious!" Tessa smiled, feeling momentarily very sophisticated. "I never knew I had such power."

"You don't!" Fran said heatedly. "Look, Tessa, my mother and your father are two very nice people. Surely they deserve a chance to find whatever happiness they can? Surely you'd allow them that?"

"I'm not against their seeing each other. Just getting married."

"Why? Because it's so final?"

The idea hadn't occurred to Tessa. It did now.

"That's it, isn't it? You still feel maybe *your* parents can patch it up."

Tessa hesitated. "That's not impossible."

"Just not very likely," Fran said.

"How do you know?" Tessa countered. "They've had

a lot of good times together. They have Allie and me."

"I don't think it has to do with you," Fran said. "But, very clearly, *they* decided—without *your* help—that it was time to move on. You can't stop progress."

"Who says it's progress?" Tessa wanted to know. "As far as I can see, they're both just at loose ends, not knowing what to do. Even my mother acts weird every once in a while, almost girlish."

"Maybe because she couldn't be that way married to your father," Fran speculated. "Maybe there were things both of them wanted to be they couldn't be if they were still married. Tessa, don't you ever give the other guy the benefit of the doubt?"

"As a matter of fact," Tessa answered, "I don't."

She turned, reached out for her mug and drained what it still held, and then started for the door of the library.

"Where are you going?" Fran demanded.

Tessa stopped, turned, and smiled wickedly. "To pee, if you don't mind," she replied slowly, letting each word out carefully and accenting the last. Then she turned again on her heel and disappeared into the living room.

15.

When I left Zandra's house, I headed straight for the museum. And straight for the little, tearful-eyed doll behind glass. When I got there, when I stood there looking up, expecting to see sympathy in her face, absolutely certain that *she* at least would understand and feel sorry for me, I couldn't see any tears. Or what I had always thought of as tears.

I moved around in front of the glass case trying to catch what I had seen before; certain that the only problem was the way the light was hitting the glass. But no matter from what angle I looked, all I saw were two almond-shaped green-flaked eyes, still looking upward but now clearly and without sorrow. Almost expectantly, if you know what I mean.

I didn't feel sad. More angry and betrayed than sad, really, and I stalked out of there and took a bus home more than ever determined to do and say and feel what I felt was true. Regardless.

My mother was *not* a terrific help.

"Tessa," she said after supper, after Allie had pulled back his bedcovers and gotten in with a book (no doubt recommended by his genius-in-residence, Ferdy Watkins), "you can't fight anymore. I don't *want* you to fight anymore."

I started to object but Mother cut me off. "Darling, listen to me for just a minute. Maybe you think, way in the back of your mind, that if Daddy stays single a while he'll come home. Out of need or desire or maybe just tiredness. But that isn't giving him the chance he deserves."

"He doesn't deserve anything," I said quickly.

My mother thought differently. "Yes, he does," she said. "And so does Zandra, no matter what you think of her. And so do I." She waited a minute before, as an after-thought it seemed to me, she said, "And so do you."

"Mother, you *love* him!"

"That's true, Tessa. I'm not denying that. And I'm not saying that watching him marry someone else is very easy. But it's something I have to do. Something I have to do *for* your father."

"Now *that* I just don't understand."

"Well, darling, there *are* a few ideas you still haven't quite the maturity to grasp."

"That's patronizing."

"It is, but it's also true," my mother said. "I'm not criticizing, Tessa. I'm not saying 'Wait till you're older.' All I am saying is that because I love your father I have to let him have his chance at a new life. And because he still loves me, in a way, he would want me to have the same chance."

"Nuts!" I said loudly.

"It's not soap opera, Tessa, believe me," Mother said.

"And I suppose you'll go to the wedding and stand there all smiles."

"No, I won't," Mother answered. "But if I'm asked, I will stop by afterwards and wish them both every happiness."

"I don't believe this," I said. "Any of it."

Mother smiled, sort of sadly I thought.

"I seem to be the only person around here who can positively see and smell disaster coming," I decided aloud. "I seem to be the only person around here who wants to do anything about it."

"You are also the only person around here who has become hard-headed, hard-nosed, and hard-hearted," my mother said. Which I thought entirely unfair.

I didn't get to sleep too easily that night. I should have, goodness knows, after a night out on the town, so to speak, in the back of that wonderful, musty old Packard. But I guess sometimes, when you hit the sack and feel *so* grateful to be there, expecting to drop off instantly for ten solid ones, sometimes you're just plainly *too tired* to relax.

Another waltz started in my head. My mother's self-lessness, which I still couldn't quite believe. (I didn't want to.) My face-off with Fran. The maddeningly reasonable way Zandra behaved. The selfishness of my father, walking out on me without even waiting to hear what I said.

Now, you might suppose that "selfishness" was the word that started everything, that began to echo and resound and pushed me toward, well, toward giving up.

In a way, it was. But not really. I thought about my father, going off to the office instead of facing me. And then I thought, well, why not? He'd heard everything I had to say. Being very honest, all I could hope to say or do ever was what Charlotte calls "variations on a theme." He did have other responsibilities. I mean, he does still have to make a living, no matter whether he's married or not. He does still have people, besides us, he has to please and satisfy. His life, actually (and this was the new thought), was bigger than just Allie and Mother and me. Or even Zandra and Fran.

I remember sitting up in bed just about then, thinking this through, and peering over at my mother. As far as one could tell, she was dead to the world. I lay back down on my pillow, doubting that she could fall asleep so quickly, suspecting deep down inside suddenly that maybe her life, too, was bigger than I had thought before. Maybe *she* was tired. Maybe *she* wanted to concentrate on something new. Even some*one* new. If I was going to harp and scream and carry on all the time, I might lose my very best audiences.

By that time, I was wide-awake. I mean *boggle-eyed*. I had stumbled on an idea that I didn't like at all.

And even though I know it's silly-sounding, I'll share it, because it makes me very uneasy.

Maybe love is only a *part* of life.

I know this sounds romantic, and actually I'm a fairly level-headed, straightforward person. But I think, well, for maybe I don't know how many years up until that very night, I had thought love was *all* of life.

I don't mean that it still couldn't be. Love for one's neighbors and friends, even for people hundreds and thousands of miles away who are, when you stop to think about it, just exactly like friends and neighbors anyway. Love of country, or love of one's fellow beings; love for one's job, one's home, one's anything.

But what I had been trying to do was make Love the most important thing in everyone's else's life, too.

And is that fair? If they don't really and truly feel that way?

My father is a mature man with duties and responsibilities, likes and dislikes, and they're all *his*. And Mother's the same. Even Zandra must have ideas and interests that don't center on Daddy or Fran.

In a way, it's what Fran said. Growing up should mean growing *out*, too. And for some reason, I was fighting that. All alone. Everyone around me—even Allie—was able to adjust, to grow with a new experience, a new environment. Only Teresa O'Connell wanted to stay tight in her snuggies, feet all wrapped up and warm, drop-seat buttoned but available.

I snuggled into my bedcovers and hugged my pillow, smiling at my own idea, which is pretty stupid. But I felt pretty stupid, if you want to know.

Another thing I thought about was when Fran said I wasn't just a baby who could cry whenever she didn't get the attention she decided she deserved. Babies do do that. I mean, they think they're the center of the universe. Everything exists for them: food, comfort, love.

Maybe I was like that.

And if love was only a part of everyone's life, then one person—one special person—even that person could ever only hope to be a *part* of someone else's life. I was only one of two kids Daddy had to watch out for. Zandra was only one woman in his life. I couldn't expect him to cut himself off from every other kind of experience with people like me, or like Mother. That just isn't realistic. Every day of his life he's going to meet new people, new women or new men, and respond to them in one fashion or another.

Now, I'm not terrifically keen on the Oedipus theory, but suddenly I caught a glimpse of myself trying to squeeze Daddy (and Allie and Mother) into my snuggies, wrapping them up very carefully and warmly, sheltering them from things *I* didn't consider good or wise or healthy.

And you can't do that. Like Charlotte says, every person has to be free to make his own mistake, no matter how stupid.

And I realized that, for myself, my father was only a part of my life, really and truly. That even *I* looked outward and saw and heard and felt things that had absolutely nothing to do with him.

It's what I said a long time ago: the one thing I hate above everything else is when someone puts an idea into your head you hadn't thought about even toying with, and then suddenly you can't get it out of your mind.

That's exactly what was happening to me.

Not that I had suddenly decided to be Pollyanna and smile and curtsey and be gracious. I mean there are ways and ways of adjusting.

I'd have to tell Mother first, of course. And then I *would* go to the wedding next week. Very pleasant I can be, too, if I want. But only that: pleasant and *aloof:* distant but serene.

I don't feel I have to try to prove to everyone that I'm positively ecstatic about things. But the least I can be is gracious. If I'm going to make my own mistakes later, there's no reason why two grown-up people can't be allowed to make their own now.

Actually, I might even be able to help Daddy and Zandra adjust to each other. After all, I'm a fairly perceptive person, and not many people know Daddy as well as I do. There are bound to be minutes or maybe even whole days when Zandra doesn't know what to make of my father's behavior. (This, of course, would be true for Fran as far as her mother goes, but I'm not quite ready to imagine Fran and me working together to help *anyone* solve *anything*.)

One thing: affection is something people earn, like friendship. The very least I can do, in my own distant but serene fashion, is give Zandra and Fran and even Daddy (again) the chance to do that. Maybe, in time, I'll even let myself respond in kind, as they say.

And as for me, for my own energies, Toby Bridgeman awaits. It's time for *me* to open up to include someone new in my life. To add another *part,* another person, to the world I already know.

One idea is rather comforting. Even if Toby Bridgeman and I manage to get along for a while, I mean, whether or not this turns out to be the love of my life, still and all from now on, Toby Bridgeman will always be a *part* of my life. It's a nice idea.

And besides, with huge sighs of relief, we're now motorized. At last.

About the Author

John Neufeld is the author of six earlier novels of distinction, including the widely praised EDGAR ALLAN, TWINK, FOR ALL THE WRONG REASONS, and LISA, BRIGHT AND DARK. The last-named became a best-selling paperback and was filmed as a Hallmark Hall of Fame television production.

Mr. Neufeld was born and raised in the Midwest and is a graduate of Phillips Exeter Academy and Yale University. After seven years in book publishing, he now devotes his full time to writing.